# Rex S ⟨✦⟩ O9-BUD-697

REX STOUT, the creator of Nero Wolfe, was born in Nobles-ville, Indiana, in 1886, the sixth of nine children of John and Lucetta Todhunter Stout, both Quakers. Shortly after his birth the family moved to Wakarusa, Kansas. He was edu-cated in a country school, but by the age of nine he was recognized throughout the state as a prodigy in arithmetic. Mr. Stout briefly attended the University of Kansas but he left to enlist in the Navy and spent the next two years as a warrant officer on board President Theodore Roosevelt's yacht. When he left the Navy in 1908, Rex Stout began to write free-lance articles and worked as a sightseeing guide and an itinerant bookkeeper. Later he devised and imple-mented a school banking system that was installed in four hundred cities and towns throughout the country. In 1927 Mr. Stout retired from the world of finance and, with the proceeds from his banking scheme, left for Paris to write serious fiction. He wrote three novels that received favorable reviews before turning to detective fiction. His first Nero Wolfe novel, *Fer-de-Lance*, appeared in 1934. It was followed by many others, among them, *Too Many Cooks, The Silent Speaker, If Death Ever Slept, The Doorbell Rang,* and *Please Pass the Guilt*, which established Nero Wolfe as a leading character on a par with Erle Stanley Gardner's famous pro-tagonist, Perry Mason. During World War II Rex Stout waged a personal campaign against Nazism as chairman of the War Writers' Board, master of ceremonies of the radio program "Speaking of Liberty," and member of several national com-mittees. After the war he turned his attention to mobilizing public opinion against the wartime use of thermonuclear de-vices, was an active leader in the Authors Guild, and re-sumed writing his Nero Wolfe novels. Rex Stout died in 1975 at the age of eighty-eight. A month before his death he pub-lished his seventy-second Nero Wolfe mystery, *A Family Af-fair*. Ten years later, a seventy-third Nero Wolfe mystery was discovered and published in *Death Times Three*.

# The Rex Stout Library

# REX STOUT

# Three for the Chair

*Introduction
by Sharyn McCrumb*

BANTAM BOOKS
NEW YORK · TORONTO · LONDON · SYDNEY · AUCKLAND

A NERO WOLFE
MYSTERY

CRIME LINE ™

THREE FOR THE CHAIR

A Bantam Crime Line Book / published by arrangement
with Viking Penguin

PUBLISHING HISTORY

Viking edition published May 1957
Bantam edition / July 1958
Bantam reissue edition / September 1994

ISBN 978-0-553-24813-5

*Published simultaneously in the United States and Canada*

Bantam Books are published by Bantam Books, a division of Random House,
Inc. Its trademark, consisting of the words "Bantam Books" and the por-
trayal of a rooster, is Registered in U.S. Patent and Trademark Office and in
other countries. Marca Registrada. Bantam Books, New York, New York

PRINTED IN THE UNITED STATES OF AMERICA

25 24 23 22

# Introduction

I wonder how an old mountain boy like Nero Wolfe ended up living in New York City.

He's originally from a central European country called *Montenegro*, you know. The word means "black mountain." It was once a republic and then part of greater Yugoslavia. Lord knows what it is now. It's about fifty miles south of Sarajevo, though. Wolfe was probably wise to leave early. Anyhow, encyclopedias describe Montenegro as wholly mountainous, with a population of less than half a million supporting themselves with sheep, goats, and forestry. Aside from wars and politics, it was probably a marvelous place to spend a childhood.

I have always felt some affinity for the reclusive Mr. Wolfe because I suspect that we have things in common: maybe some folk tales and fiddle tunes, but certainly a way of looking at the world. His mountains are part of the Carpathian chain, while mine are the southern Appalachians of east Tennessee and southwest Virginia, but there is a universal kinship among mountain people. They have the same ways of doing things: a love of nature and a dislike for authority; a fierce pride and a stubborn streak. And although they are loyal and hospitable, they tend to be wary of strangers. I'm pretty sure there's a word in Serbo-Croatian for *hillbilly*.

For years people have called Nero Wolfe eccentric and strange because he refuses to leave his Manhattan brownstone, because he grows orchids on the roof of his building, and because he's not a sociable, glad-handing fellow. This just goes to show that you can take a man out of the mountains but not vice-versa, because, given his situation, Nero Wolfe is behaving in a perfectly reasonable fashion—for a city-bound mountaineer.

A friend of mine who grew up in the coves of eastern Kentucky got an education and an important job late in life, and he made his first trip to New York City when he was well past forty. When Garry got back to Kentucky after two weeks in Manhattan, I called him up and asked how he liked the Big Apple. There was a pronounced pause at the end of the telephone line, and then he said, "Did you know there're people who go there *on purpose?*" I am certain that if my friend Garry or Spencer Arrowood, the Tennessee sheriff in my Ballad novels, were forced to stay in New York City longer than a few weeks, they, too, would be holed up in a brownstone, refusing to come out and confront that teeming mass of strangers.

And if Sheriff Arrowood had to stay in a concrete holler in midtown, he'd be growing anything that would take root up there on the roof, just out of home-sickness for greenery. He would gather a family of sorts about him, just as Nero Wolfe has assembled a clan consisting of Archie, Fritz, Theodore, and Saul Panzer; and he would be as fiercely loyal to them as Wolfe is to his folks—though there might be some infighting when their egos rubbed together. Apologies would be rare.

When Nero Wolfe comes out of his brownstone lair, it's for one of two reasons: authority (which he doesn't like) has forced him out, or he's going to the country. In *Three for the Chair* we have examples of both. In the novella "Too Many Detectives" Wolfe and Archie are summoned to the state capital for a wire-tapping investigation, and Wolfe is at his irascible and uncooperative best with the Albany version of "reve-nuers." In "Immune to Murder" Wolfe heads for the mountains—the Adirondacks—to cook brook trout for visiting diplomats.

Wolfe has all the good qualities of mountain people, as well as their solitary ways. He is whip-smart, honorable, and quite capable of adapting to the customs of the cultural elite. People underestimate Nero Wolfe—and the rest of us mountain folk—at their peril. We can jettison the accent, acquire a taste for opera and sushi, and stifle the glower of Wolfe under the sparkle of Archie's charm and self-deprecating humor. Most of us feel like Wolfe but have to act like Archie. We manage. But we tend to count trees when nobody's looking, and we always, always hold something back. Inside each of us there's a brownstone fortress, and it takes some doing to get us out of it.

Nero Wolfe has outlived his creator, and even now he is practicing the art of detection from his Manhattan home; but if he *had* been allowed to retire, I think I'd see another mountain trait in him. I saw it in my great-uncles, who spent forty years between youth and retirement working in the car factories in Detroit. When their working lives came to an end, they went back to the mountains. The lucky ones never leave; the rest come home when they can. Wolfe settled in

New York because you can't be an eminent and well-paid private detective in, say, Banner Elk, North Carolina; but for all Wolfe's success, I am not convinced that he felt at home in the city. I think his residence there would have ended when he quit the gumshoe business.

Maybe Nero Wolfe wouldn't have made it all the way back to the hills of Montenegro, but if he'd ever been allowed to stop crime solving, I think I'd know where to look for him. You'd be walking on the Appalachian Trail, in the green wilderness somewhere between Springer Mountain, Georgia and Mount Katahdin, Maine, and as you started to climb over a split-rail fence to reach a spring, a voice would yell, "Get away from my rhododendrons!" And you'd see a pear-shaped hulk glowering down at you from the deck of a glass and cedar chalet up on the ridge. Walk softly, dear reader. Archie's no doubt somewhere on the premises. He's probably armed. Now git.

—Sharyn McCrumb

# Contents

# A Window
# for Death

Nero Wolfe, behind his desk, sat glaring at the caller in the red leather chair. I was swiveled with my back to my desk, ready with my notebook, not glaring.

Wolfe's glare was partly on general principles, but more because David R. Fyfe had not phoned for an appointment. You might think it didn't matter. There was the office, on the ground floor of the old brownstone house on West 35th Street. There was Wolfe in the chair he loved, sharpening his penknife on the old oilstone he kept in a drawer. There was I, Archie Goodwin, eager to earn my pay by serving his slightest whim, within reason. There was Fritz Brenner in the kitchen, doing the luncheon dishes, set to bring beer if the buzzer went one short and one long. There was Theodore Horstmann up in the plant rooms on the roof, nursing the ten thousand orchids. And there in the red leather chair was a guy who wanted to hire a detective or he wouldn't have come. But for him and others like him Fritz and Theodore and I would have been out looking for jobs, and God only knows what Wolfe would have been doing. But Wolfe was glaring at him. He should have phoned for an appointment.

He sat forward in the red leather chair, not touch-

ing the back, his narrow shoulders sagging and his
pale narrow face looking the worse for wear. I would
have guessed his age at fifty, but most people look
older than they are when forced by circumstances to
go to a private detective. In a tired, careful voice,
after giving his name and address and his occupation
—head of the English Department at Audubon High
School in the Bronx—he said he wanted Wolfe to investigate a confidential family matter.

"Marital?" Wolfe made a noise that went with the
glare. "No."

He shook his head. "It isn't marital. I am a widower, with two children in high school. It's about my
brother Bertram—his death. He died Saturday night
of pneumonia. It will have to be—I'll have to explain
about it."

Wolfe sent me a glance, and I met it. If he let Fyfe
explain he might have to work, and he hated to work,
especially when the bank balance was healthy. But I
tightened my lips a little as I met his glance, and he
sighed and went back to the customer. "Do so," he
muttered.

Fyfe did so, and I took it down. His brother Bertram had suddenly appeared in New York a month
ago, unannounced, after an absence of twenty years,
and taken an apartment in the Churchill Towers, and
communicated with his family—his older brother,
David, who was doing the explaining, his younger
brother, Paul, and his sister, Louise, now Mrs. Vincent Tuttle. They had all been glad to see him again
after so many years, including Tuttle, the brother-in-
law, and had also been glad to learn that he had hit a
jack pot—not David's word, his was bonanza—by
finding and hooking onto a four-mile lode of uranium
ore near a place called Black Elbow somewhere in

Canada. It is always nice to know that a member of the family has made out well.

So they had welcomed Bertram, their brother Bert, and along with him a young man named Johnny Arrow who had accompanied him from Canada and was living with him in the Churchill Towers apartment. Bert had been fairly fraternal and had shown an interest in old memories and associations; he had even asked Paul, who was a real-estate broker, to get a line on the purchase of the old house in Mount Kisco where they had all been born and spent their childhood. Obviously Bert was back as one of the family. Ten days ago he had invited them to dine with him on Saturday the sixth, and afterwards go to the theater, but on Thursday he had been put to bed with pneumonia. He refused to go to a hospital, and insisted that they should dine at the Churchill as planned and use the theater tickets, so they gathered at his apartment late Saturday afternoon and carried out the program, returning to the apartment after the show for a champagne snack.

That is, four of them did—sister Louise and her husband, Johnny Arrow from Canada, and brother David himself. Younger brother Paul had maintained that Bert shouldn't be left alone with the nurse, and had stayed at the apartment. When the four returned after the show they found a situation. Paul had gone and the nurse had a torn uniform and marks on her neck and cheeks and wrists. She had phoned the doctor to send another nurse and intended to leave as soon as her replacement came. Sister Louise resented some of her remarks and ordered her to leave at once, and she went. Louise phoned the doctor and told him she would stay until another nurse came. Johnny Arrow disappeared, leaving only David and Louise and

her husband, Vincent Tuttle, on the scene; and after
David had looked in at Bert on his sickbed, sound
asleep under the morphine the nurse had given him
by doctor's orders he departed for home.

Louise and Tuttle went to bed in a room that was
presumably Johnny Arrow's, but were not yet asleep
when a buzz took Tuttle to the door of the apartment,
where he found Paul. Paul said he had been assaulted
by Johnny Arrow down in the men's bar, and had an
assortment of bruises to show as evidence. Arrow had
been escorted away by two cops. Paul thought his jaw
was broken and possibly a rib or two, and he didn't
feel like driving home to Mount Kisco, so they put him
on a couch in the living room, and in thirty seconds he
was snoring, and after another glance in at the door of
Bert's room Louise and Tuttle went back to bed.
Around six in the morning they were aroused by
Paul. He had aroused himself by tumbling off the
couch, had gone to look at Bert, and had found him
dead. They phoned down to the desk for a doctor because Bert had insisted on having the old family doctor he knew in his boyhood, and they didn't want to
wait for him to get in from Mount Kisco. Of course
they phoned him too, and he got there later.

Wolfe was fidgeting. He fidgets by making circles
the size of a dime with a fingertip on his chair arm. "I
trust," he grumbled, "that the doctors will now justify
your calling on me and this long recital. Or at least
one of them."

"No, sir." David Fyfe shook his head. "They found
nothing wrong. My brother died of pneumonia. Doctor
Buhl—that's the one from Mount Kisco, Doctor Frederick Buhl—he signed the death certificate, and my
brother was buried Monday, yesterday, in the family
plot. Of course the nurse having gone made the—uh—

the situation was a little embarrassing, but no serious question was raised."

"Then what the devil do you want of me?"

"I'm about to tell you." Fyfe cleared his throat, and when he went on his voice was more careful than ever. "After the funeral yesterday that man Arrow asked us to come to the apartment at eleven o'clock this morning to hear the will read, and of course we went. Louise brought her husband along. There was a lawyer there, a man named McNeil who had flown down from Montreal, and he had the will. It had all the usual legal rigmarole, but what it amounted to was that Bert left his whole estate to Paul and Louise and me, and made that man Arrow the executor. It put no value on the estate, but from things Bert had said I would have thought his uranium holdings were worth upwards of five million dollars, possibly twice that."

Wolfe stopped fidgeting.

"Then," Fyfe went on, "the lawyer took another document from his brief case. He said it was a copy of an agreement he had drawn up a year ago for Bertram Fyfe and Johnny Arrow. He read it. There was a preamble about their prospecting together for uranium for five years, and their joint discovery of the Black Elbow lode, and the gist of it was that if either of them died the whole thing would become the property of the survivor, including any assets that had been acquired by the deceased through income from the mining property. That wasn't the phraseology, it was all very legal, but that's what it meant. As soon as he read it Johnny Arrow spoke up. He said that Bert had possessed nothing that had not been acquired with income from the Black Elbow uranium, and that therefore it was now legally his property, including large sums on deposit in Canadian banks, but that when Bert came to New York he had had some thirty or forty thousand dollars transferred to a New York bank, and he, Arrow, didn't intend to claim what was left of it. That would be the estate and we could have it."

David made a mild little gesture. "He was being generous, I thought, since he could have claimed that too. We asked the lawyer a few questions and then left and went out to a restaurant for lunch. Paul was raging. My brother Paul is impulsive. He wanted to go to the police and tell them Bert had died in suspicious circumstances, and ask them to investigate. His theory was that when Arrow saw that Bert was getting reconciled with his family he was afraid he might make large gifts to us, possibly even a share of the mining properties, and Arrow couldn't claim them under the agreement if Bert died, so he decided he had to die now. Vincent Tuttle, my sister's husband, objected that even if the theory was sound Arrow hadn't acted on it, since two competent doctors had agreed that Bert had died of pneumonia, and Louise and I agreed with him, but Paul was stubborn. He hinted that he knew something we didn't know, but then he has always liked to be a little mysterious. He stuck to it that we should go to the police, and we argued about it, and finally I suggested a compromise. I suggested that I get Nero Wolfe to investigate, and if you decided there was sufficient reason to call in the police we would join with Paul in doing so, and if you decided there wasn't, Paul would forget it. Paul said all right, he would accept your decision, so that's what I want you to do. I know you charge high fees, but this shouldn't require any great—uh—I mean it shouldn't be too complicated. It's a fairly simple problem, isn't it?"

Wolfe grunted. "It could be. There was no autopsy?"

"No, no. Good heavens, no."

"That should be the first step, but it's too late now, without the police. Before burial an examination could have been made merely to satisfy medical curiosity, but exhumation needs authority. I take it that you want me to investigate, and reach a decision, without attracting the attention of the police."

Fyfe nodded emphatically. "That's right. That's exactly right. We don't want any scandal . . . any rumors going around . . ."

"People rarely do," Wolfe said drily. "But you may be hiring me to start one. You understand, of course, that if I find evidence of skulduggery it will not be in your sole discretion whether to bury it or disclose it. I will not engage to suppress grounds, if I find any, for a suspicion of homicide. If my investigation results in a reasonable assumption that you have yourself committed a crime, I am free to act as I see fit."

"Of course." Fyfe tried to smile, with fair success. "Only I know I have committed no crime, and I doubt if any one has. My brother Paul is a little impetuous. You'll need to see him, naturally, and he'll want to see you."

"I'll have to see all of them." Wolfe's tone was morose. Work. He grabbed at a straw: "But under the circumstances I must ask for a retainer as a token of good faith. Say a check for a thousand dollars?"

It wasn't a bad try, since a head of a high-school English department with two children might not have a grand lying around loose, and the deal would have been off, but Fyfe didn't even attempt to haggle. He did gulp, and gulped again after he got out a check folder and pen and wrote, and signed his name. I got up and accepted the check when he offered it, and passed it across to Wolfe.

"It's a little steep," Fyfe said—not a complaint, just a fact—"but it can't be helped. It's the only way to satisfy Paul. When will you see him?"

Wolfe gave the check a look and put it under a paperweight, a chunk of petrified wood that had once been used by a man named Duggan to crack his wife's skull. He glanced up at the wall clock; in twenty minutes it would be four o'clock, time for his afternoon session in the plant rooms.

"First," he told Fyfe, "I need to speak with Doctor Buhl. Can you have him here at six o'clock?"

David looked doubtful. "I could try. He would have to come in from Mount Kisco, and he's a busy man. Can't you leave him out of it? He certified the death, and he's thoroughly reputable."

"It's impossible to leave him out. I must see him before dealing with the others. If he can be here at six, arrange for the others to come at six-thirty. Your brother and sister, and Mr. Tuttle, and Mr. Arrow."

Fyfe stared. "Good heavens," he protested, "not Arrow! Anyway, he wouldn't come." He shook his head emphatically. "No. I won't ask him."

Wolfe shrugged. "Then I will. And it might be better—yes. It may be protracted, and I dine at seven-thirty. If you can arrange for Doctor Buhl to be here at nine, bring the others at half past. That will give us the night if we need it. Of course, Mr. Fyfe, there are several points I could go into with you now—for instance, the situation you found when you returned to the apartment from the theater, and your brother Bertram's reconciliation with his family—but I have an appointment; and besides, they can be explored more fully this evening. For the present, please give Mr. Goodwin the addresses and phone numbers of everyone involved." He moved his vast bulk forward in his chair to pick up the penknife and start rubbing it gently on the oilstone. He had undertaken that job, and by gum he intended to finish it.

"I described the situation," Fyfe said in a sharper tone. "I invited the inference that Paul had stayed at the apartment in order to approach the nurse. I wholly disapprove of his method of approaching women. I have said he is impetuous."

Wolfe was feeling the knife's edge tenderly with a thumb.

"What is the point," Fyfe asked, "about the reconciliation?"

"Only that you used the word." Wolfe was honing again. "What needed to be reconciled? It may be irrelevant, but so are most points raised in an investigation. It can wait till this evening."

Fyfe was frowning. "It's an old sore," he said, the sharpness gone and his voice tired again. "It may not be irrelevant, because it may partly account for Paul's attitude. Also I suppose we're over-sensitive about any threat of scandal. Pneumonia is a touchy subject with us. My father died of pneumonia twenty years ago, but it was thought by the police he was murdered. Not only by the police. He was in a ground-floor bedroom in our house at Mount Kisco, and it was January, and on a stormy night, extremely cold, someone raised two windows and left them wide open. I found him dead at five o'clock in the morning. Snow was drifted a foot deep on the floor and there was snow on the bed. My sister Louise, who was caring for him that night, was sound asleep on a couch in the next room. It was thought that some hot chocolate she drank at midnight had been drugged, but that wasn't proven. The windows weren't locked and could have been opened from the outside—in fact, they must have been. My father had been a little shrewd in some of his real-estate dealings, and there were people in the community who had been—uh—who were not fond of him."

Fyfe repeated the mild little gesture. "So you see, there is the coincidence. Unfortunately, my brother Bert—he was only twenty-two then—he had quarreled with my father and was not living at home. He was living in a rooming house about a mile away and had a job in a garage. The police thought they had enough evidence to arrest him for murder, and he was tried, but the evidence certainly wasn't conclusive, because he was acquitted. Anyhow he had an alibi. Up to two o'clock that night he had been playing cards with a friend—Vincent Tuttle, who later married my sister—in Tuttle's room in the rooming house, and it had stopped snowing shortly after two, and the windows must have been opened long before it stopped snowing. But Bert resented some of our testimony on the witness stand—Paul's and Louise's and mine—though all we did was tell the truth about things that were known anyway—for example, Bert's quarrel with my father. Everybody knew about it. The day after he was acquitted Bert left town, and we never heard from him, not a word for twenty years. So that's why I used the word 'reconciled.'"

Wolfe had returned the knife to his pocket and was putting the oilstone in the drawer.

"Actually," Fyfe said, "Arrow was wrong when he stated that Bert possessed nothing that had not been acquired with income from the uranium. Bert never claimed his share of our father's estate, and they couldn't find him, and we have never applied for its distribution. His one-quarter share was around sixty thousand dollars, and now it's more than double that. Of course Paul and Louise and I will get it now, but honestly it will give me no pleasure. I may say frankly, Mr. Wolfe, that I am sorry Bert came back. It reopened an old sore, and now his death, and the way it happened, and Paul acting like this . . ."

It was one minute to four, and Wolfe was pushing his chair back and leaving it. "Yes indeed, Mr. Fyfe," he concurred. "A nuisance alive and an affliction dead. Please give Mr. Goodwin the necessary information, and phone when you have made the arrangements for this evening."

He headed for the door.

## II

A little research into backgrounds is often a help, even in cases that apparently don't call for it, and after Fyfe left I made a few phone calls to various quarters, getting a skimpy crop of useless information. David had taught at Audubon High School for twelve years, and had been head of the English Department for four. Paul's real estate agency in Mount Kisco was no whirlwind but was seemingly solvent. Vincent Tuttle's drugstore, also in Mount Kisco, was his own, and was thought to be doing fine. David had had no address or phone number for the nurse, Anne Goren, but Wolfe wanted them all, and I found her in the Manhattan book, listed as an RN. The first two times I dialed her number I got a busy signal, and the next

three times no answer. Nor could I get Johnny Arrow. Calls to the Churchill Towers go through the
Churchill switchboard, and I left word for him to call,
and made half a dozen tries. Finally, just before Fritz
announced dinner, I got Tim Evarts, assistant house
dick, security officer to you, and asked him a few discreet questions. The answers were both for and
against. For, the rent was paid on the de luxe Towers
apartment, and the bar and restaurant staff all liked
Johnny Arrow, especially his tipping standards.
Against, Arrow had plugged a guy in the bar Saturday night, repeatedly and persistently, and had been
removed by cops. Tim said that technically it had been
a fine performance, but the Churchill bar wasn't the
place for it.

Fyfe had phoned that the arrangements had been
made. At nine o'clock, when Doctor Frederick Buhl
arrived, Wolfe and I were through in the dining room,
having put away around four pounds of salmon
mousse, Wolfe's own recipe, and a peck of summer
salad, and were back in the office. The doorbell took
me to the hall, and as I switched on the stoop light
what I saw through the one-way glass panel of the
front door gave me a double surprise. Doctor Buhl, if
it was he, was no doddering old worn-out hick doc; he
was an erect, gray-haired, well-dressed man of distinction. And with him was a young female having her
own personal points of distinction, discernible even by
a swift glance at a distance.

I went and opened up. He moved aside for her to
enter and then followed, saying that he was Doctor
Buhl and had an appointment with Nero Wolfe. No
hat covered his crown of distinguished gray hair, so
there was nothing for the rack, and I led them down
the hall and into the office. Inside, he halted to dart a

glance around, then crossed to Wolfe's desk and said aggressively, "I'm Frederick Buhl. David Fyfe asked me to come. What is all this nonsense?"

"I don't know," Wolfe murmured. He keeps his voice down to a murmur after a meal, unless goaded. "I've been hired to find out. Sit down, sir. The young woman?"

"She's the nurse. Miss Anne Goren. Sit down, Anne."

She was already sitting, in a chair I had moved up for her. I was making revisions in my opinion of Paul Fyfe. Probably he had been too impetuous, but the temptation had been strong; and the marks on her neck and cheeks and wrists must have been superficial since no scars were visible. Also a nurse's uniform is much more provocative than the blue cotton print she was wearing, with a bolero jacket to match. Even in the cotton print, I could have—but skip it. She was there on business. She thanked me for the chair, coldly, no smile.

Doctor Buhl, in the red leather chair, demanded, "Well, what is it?"

Wolfe murmured, "Didn't Mr. Fyfe tell you?"

"He told me that Paul thought there was something suspicious about Bert's death and wanted to go to the police, and David and Louise and Vincent Tuttle couldn't talk him out of it, and they agreed to get you to investigate and accept your decision, and he had talked with you, and you insisted on seeing me. I think it quite unnecessary. I am a reputable physician, and I signed a death certificate."

"So I understand," Wolfe murmured. "But if my decision is to be final it should be well fortified. I have no thought of challenging the propriety of your issuance of the death certificate. But there are a few questions. When did you last see Bertram Fyfe alive?"

"Saturday evening. I was there half an hour, and left at twenty minutes past seven. The others were there, having dinner in the living room. He had refused to go to a hospital. I had put him under an oxygen tent, but he kept jerking it off, he wouldn't have it. I couldn't get him to leave it on, and neither could Miss Goren. He was in considerable pain, or said he was, but his temperature was down to a hundred and two. He was a difficult patient. He couldn't sleep, and I told the nurse to give him a quarter of a grain of morphine as soon as the guests had gone, and another quarter-grain an hour later if that didn't work—he had had half a grain the night before."

"Then you returned to Mount Kisco?"

"Yes."

"Did you think he might die that night?"

"Of course not."

"Then when you got word Sunday morning that he was dead, weren't you surprised?"

"Of course I was." Buhl flattened his palms on the chair arms. "Mr. Wolfe, I am tolerating this as a favor to David Fyfe. You are being inane. I'm sixty years old. I've been practising medicine for more than thirty years, and fully half of my patients have surprised me one way or another—by bleeding too much or too little, by getting a rash from taking aspirin, by refusing to show a temperature with a high blood count, by living when they should die, by dying when they should have lived. That is the universal experience of general practitioners. Yes, Bertram Fyfe's death was a surprise, but it was by no means unprecedented. I examined the body with great care a few hours after he died, and found nothing whatever to make me question the cause of death. So I issued the certificate."

"Why did you examine the body with great care?" Wolfe was still murmuring.

"Because the nurse had left him in the middle of the night—had been forced to leave—and I hadn't been able to get a replacement. The best I could do was to arrange for one to report at seven in the morning. Under those circumstances I thought it well to make a thorough examination for the record."

"And you are completely satisfied that pneumonia was the cause of death, with no contributing factors?"

"No, of course not. Complete satisfaction is a rarity in my profession, Mr. Wolfe. But I am satisfied that it was proper and correct to issue the certificate, that it was consistent with all the observable evidence, that—in layman's language—Bertram Fyfe died of pneumonia. I am not quibbling. Long ago a patient of mine died of pneumonia, but it was a cold winter night and someone had opened the windows of his room and let the storm in. But in this case it was a hot summer night and the windows were closed. The apartment was air-conditioned, and I had instructed the nurse to keep the regulator at eighty in that room because a pneumonia patient needs warmth, and she had done so. In the case I mentioned, windows open to a winter storm were certainly a contributing factor, but in this case there was no evidence of any such factor."

Wolfe nodded approvingly. "You have covered the point admirably, doctor, but you have also raised one. The air-conditioner. What if someone moved the regulator, after the nurse's departure, to its lowest extreme? Could it have cooled the room sufficiently to cause your patient to die when you expected him to live?"

"I would say no. I considered that possibility. Mr. and Mrs. Tuttle have assured me that they did not touch the regulator and that the room's temperature remained equable, and anyway on so hot a night the conditioner couldn't have cooled the air to that extent. I wanted to be satisfied on that point, since no nurse had been there, and I arranged with the hotel to check it Saturday night, in that room. After the regulator had been at its extreme for six hours, the temperature was sixty-nine—too low for a pneumonia patient, even one well covered, but certainly not lethal."

"I see," Wolfe murmured. "You did not rely on the assurance of Mr. and Mrs. Tuttle."

Buhl smiled. "Is that quite fair? I relied on them as wholly as you rely on me. I was being thorough. I am thorough."

"An excellent habit. I have it too. Did you have any suspicion, with or without reason, that someone might have contrived to help the pneumonia kill your patient?"

"No. I was merely being thorough."

Wolfe nodded. "Well." He heaved a deep sigh, and when it had been disposed of turned his head to focus on the nurse. During the conversation she had sat with her back straight, her chin up, and her hands folded in her lap. I had her profile. There are not many female chins that rate high both from the front and from the side.

Wolfe spoke. "One question, Miss Goren—or two. Do you concur with all that Doctor Buhl has told me— all that you have knowledge of?"

"Yes, I do." Her voice was a little husky, but she hadn't been using it.

"I understand that while the others were at the theater Paul Fyfe made advances to you which you repulsed. Is that correct?"

"Yes."

"Did that cause you to neglect your duties in any way? Did it interfere with your proper care of your patient?"

"No. The patient was sound asleep, under sedation."

"Have you any comment or information to offer? I have been hired by David Fyfe to determine whether anything about his brother's death warrants a police inquiry. Can you tell me anything whatever that might help me decide?"

Her eyes left him to go to Buhl, then came back again. "No, I can't," she said. She stood up. Of course nurses are expected to rise from a chair without commotion, but she just floated up. "Is that all?"

Wolfe didn't reply, and she moved. Buhl got to his feet. But when she was half way to the door Wolfe called, considerably above a murmur, "Miss Goren! One moment!" She turned to look at him. "Sit down, please?" he invited her.

She hesitated, glanced at Buhl, and came back to the chair. "Yes?" she asked.

Wolfe regarded her briefly, and then turned to Buhl. "I could have asked you before," he said, "why you brought Miss Goren. It seemed quite unnecessary, since you were fully prepared and qualified to deal with me, and surely it was inconsiderate to drag her into a matter so delicate. It was a reasonable inference that you expected me to ask some question that she could answer and you couldn't, so you had to have her with you. Evidently I didn't ask it, but I did provoke her. When I asked if she could tell me anything she looked at you. Manifestly she is withholding something, and you know what it is. I can't pump it out of you, with no bribe to offer and no threat to brandish, but my curiosity has been aroused and must somehow be satisfied. You may prefer to satisfy it yourself."

Buhl had sat and, his elbow on the chair arm, was pulling at his fine straight nose with a thumb and forefinger. He let his hand drop. "You're not just a windbag," he said. "You're quite correct. I expected you to bring up something that would require Miss Goren's presence, and I'm astonished that you didn't. I wanted to consider it, but I'm perfectly willing to bring it up myself. Haven't they mentioned the hot-water bags to you?"

"No, sir. I have been told nothing about hot-water bags."

"Then I suppose Paul—but it doesn't matter what I suppose. Tell him about it, Anne."

"He already knows about it," she said scornfully. "One of them hired him."

"Tell me anyway," Wolfe suggested, "for comparison." His method with women is neither Paul's nor mine.

"Very well." Her lovely chin was up. "I was keeping two hot-water bags on the patient, one on each side of his chest, and changing the water every two hours. I changed it just before I left—before Mrs. Tuttle ordered me to leave. Sunday evening Paul Fyfe came to my apartment—I have a little apartment on Forty-eighth Street with a friend, another nurse. He said that when he found his brother was dead that morning he pulled the covers down, and the hot-water bags were there, but they were empty, and he took them and put them in the bathroom. Later his sister, Mrs. Tuttle, saw them and called him to look at them and said the nurse had neglected to fill them, and she was going to report it to the doctor. He asked if she hadn't changed the water herself before she went to bed, and she said no, she hadn't thought is was necessary because the nurse had changed it just before she left."

Miss Goren's voice wasn't husky now. It was clear and firm and positive. "He said that he had told his sister that when he took the bags to the bathroom he had emptied the water out of them. He said he told her that on the spur of the moment, to keep her from reporting me to the doctor, but he had realized since that perhaps he shouldn't have told her that because the empty bags might have had something to do with his brother's death, and he asked me to go and have dinner with him so we could talk it over. We were standing at the door of the apartment, I hadn't let him in, and I slammed the door in his face. The next day, yesterday, he phoned three times, and last evening he came to the apartment again, but I didn't open the door. So he told his brother David and got him to come to you. How does it compare?"

Wolfe was frowning at her. "Pfui," he said, and gave her up and turned to Buhl. "So that's it," he growled.

Buhl nodded. "Miss Goren phoned to tell me about it Sunday evening, and again yesterday, and again last night. Naturally, since her professional competence was in question. Do you wonder that I expected you to bring it up?"

"No indeed. But I hadn't heard of it. How much

chance is there that Miss Goren did in fact fail to put water in the bags?"

"None whatever, since she says she put it in. She trained at the Mount Kisco Hospital, and I know her well. I always use her, if she's available, when I have a patient in New York. That can be eliminated."

"Then either Paul Fyfe is lying, or someone took the bags from the bed, emptied them, and put them back. Which seems senseless. Certainly it could have had no appreciable effect on the patient. Could it?"

"No. Appreciable, no." Buhl passed a palm over his distinguished gray hair. "But it could have an effect on Miss Goren's professional reputation, and I feel some responsibility. I put her on the case. You haven't asked me for an opinion, but I offer one. I think Bertram Fyfe died of pneumonia, with no contributing factors except those he contributed himself—his refusal to go to a hospital, his rejection of the oxygen tent, perhaps his capricious insistence on having them come to dinner despite his illness. He was a headstrong boy, and apparently he never changed. As for the hot-water bags, I think Paul Fyfe is lying. I don't want to slander him, but the vagaries of his conduct with women are common knowledge in his home community. A woman who strikes his fancy doesn't merely attract him; he is obsessed. It would be consonant with his former known behavior if, seeing the bags in the bed, he had formed the notion of acquiring a weapon to use on Miss Goren and took the bags to the bathroom and emptied them."

"Then," Wolfe objected, "he was an ass to tell his sister he had emptied them."

Buhl shook his head. "Only to sidetrack her. He could tell Miss Goren he had done her that service, and at the same time could threaten, at least tacitly, to disclose her negligence. I don't say he wasn't an ass; obsessed people usually are. I merely say that I think he told his sister the truth and told Miss Goren a lie. I think he emptied the bags himself. I understand he will be here this evening, with the others, and I ask you to let them know that any attempt to charge Miss Goren with an act of negligence will be deeply resented by me and strongly opposed. I will advise her to bring an action for slander and will support it. If you prefer that I tell them myself—"

The doorbell rang. I got up and went to the hall for a look, and stepped back in.

"They're here," I told Wolfe. "David and two men and a woman."

He looked up at the clock. "Ten minutes late. Bring them in."

"No!" Anne Goren was on her feet. "I won't! I won't be in a room with them! Doctor Buhl! Please!"

I must say I agreed with her. I wasn't obsessed, but I absolutely agreed. After a second's hesitation Buhl did too, and told Wolfe so. Wolfe looked at her, and decided to make it unanimous.

"All right," he conceded. "Archie, take Miss Goren and Doctor Buhl to the front room, and after the others are in here let them out."

"Yes, sir." As I went to open the door to the front room the bell rang again. Paul being impetuous. If he had known who was there he would probably have bounded through the glass panel.

## III

The way it looked to me, as I sat at my desk and got out my notebook after ushering the newcomers in and letting Buhl and Anne Goren out, an investigation of a death that had surprised the doctor was about to deteriorate into an inquiry about a real-estate agent's methods of courtship—not the sort of job that Wolfe would ever consider worthy of his genius, fee or no fee, and I was looking forward to it.

In appearance Paul was not up to his billing. He was a good eight inches shorter than me, broad and a little pudgy, and probably thought he looked like Napoleon—and maybe he did a little, or would have without the shiner (left eye) and the bruises on both sides of his swollen jaw. Evidently Johnny Arrow used both fists. Paul and the Tuttles were on chairs lined up in front of Wolfe's desk, leaving the red leather chair to David.

Louise was taller than either of her brothers, and better-looking. For a middle-aged woman she wasn't a bad sight at all, though a little bony, and her hair was too short. As for her husband, Tuttle, he was simply short of hair. His shiny dome, rising to a peak, dominated the scene and made such details as eyes and nose and chin unimportant. You had to concentrate to take them in.

When I came back and sat after letting Buhl and Anne Goren out, Wolfe was speaking. ". . . and Doctor Buhl stated that in his opinion your brother died of pneumonia, with no suspicious circumstances. Since he had already certified the death, that leaves us where we were." He focused on Paul. "I understand that you maintain that the police should be asked to investigate. Is that correct?"

"Yes. You're damn right it is." He had a baritone and gave it plenty of breath.

"And the others disagree." Wolfe's head moved. "You disagree, sir?"

"As I told you." David looked and sounded tireder than ever. "Yes, I disagree."

"And you, Mrs. Tuttle?"

"I certainly do." She was a word-clipper, with a high thin voice. "I don't believe in asking for trouble. Neither does my husband." Her head jerked sideways. "Vince?"

"That's right, my dear," Tuttle rumbled. "I always agree with you, even when I don't. This time I do."

Wolfe went back to Paul. "Then it seems to be up to you. If you go to the police what do you tell them?"

"I tell them plenty." The ceiling light made Paul's shiner look worse than it really was. "I tell them that when Doctor Buhl left Saturday evening he told us that Bert's condition was satisfactory and we could go and enjoy the play, and a few hours later Bert was dead. I tell them that that guy Arrow was making a play for the nurse, and she was giving him the eye, and he could have had an opportunity to get at her stuff and substitute something for the morphine she was going to shoot into Bert. Doctor Buhl told us he was giving morphine. I tell them that Arrow stands to rake in several million bucks that he never would have got a smell of as long as Bert was alive. I tell them that Arrow saw that Bert was getting on with us, one of the family again, and he didn't like it and showed he didn't."

Paul stopped to press gently at his jaw with fingertips. "It hurts me to talk," he said. "The goddam hoodlum. Look, I'm no prince. The way you're looking at me, you might be asking am I my brother's keeper, and hell no. I didn't get along any too well with Bert when we were kids, and I hadn't seen him for twenty years, so what. I might as well tell you what. A murderer can't collect on his crime, and if Arrow killed him that agreement is out the window, and it will all be in Bert's estate, and it will be ours. That's obvious, so why not say it? I won't have to tell the police that because they'll know it."

"That's no way to talk, Paul," David said sharply.

"That's right," Tuttle agreed. "It certainly isn't."

"Oh, can it," Paul told his brother-in-law. "Who are you?"

"He's my husband," Louise snapped at him. "He could teach you a lot of things if you were teachable."

All in the family. Wolfe took over. "I concede," he told Paul, "that you might stir the police into curiosity, but surmise is not enough. Have you anything else to tell them?"

"No. I don't need anything else."

"For me you do." Wolfe leaned back, pulled in a bushel of air, and let it out again. "Let's see if we can find something. What time did you arrive at your brother's apartment Saturday evening?"

"Saturday afternoon around five o'clock." The bottom half of Paul's face was suddenly contorted, and I thought he was having a spasm until I realized he was merely trying to grin, which is a problem with a sore jaw. "I get it," he said, "where was I at nine minutes to six on August sixth? Okay. I left Mount Kisco at a quarter to four, alone in my car, and drove to New York. My first stop was at Schramm's on Madison Avenue, to buy two quarts of their mango ice cream to take back to Mount Kisco for a Sunday party. Then I

drove to Fifty-second Street and parked the car,
which can be done on a Saturday afternoon, and
walked to the Churchill, arriving at the apartment a
little after five. I went early because I had spoken
with the nurse on the phone and liked her voice, and I
thought I might get acquainted with her before the
others came. Not a chance. That guy Arrow had her
in the living room, telling her about prospecting for
uranium. Every ten minutes or so she would sneak in
for a look at her patient and then come back for more
about prospecting. Then Dave came, and then Louise
and Vince, and we were just starting dinner around a
quarter to seven when Doctor Buhl came. Want
more?"

"You might as well finish."

"Anything you say. Buhl was in with Bert about
half an hour, and when he left—I told you what he
told us. We not only ate, we drank, and maybe I
overdid it a little. I thought it wouldn't be right to
leave the nurse alone with Bert, and when the others
left to go to the show I stayed. I thought if the nurse
liked to hear about prospecting she might like to hear
about other things too, but apparently not. After a
little—oh, some remarks back and forth—she went in
Bert's room and shut the door and locked it. She told
my sister later that I banged on the door and yelled at
her that if she didn't come out I'd break the door
down, but I don't remember it that way. Anyhow, by
that time Bert was dead to the world with morphine,
if it was morphine. She did come out, and we talked,
and I may have touched her, but the marks on her
that she showed them when they got back from the
theater—she must have done that herself. I wasn't
that drunk, I was just a little high. Finally she got at
the phone and said if I didn't leave she would call

down to the desk and tell them to send someone up, and I beat it. Want more?"

"Go ahead."

"Righto. I went down to the bar and sat at a table and had a drink. Two or three drinks. Something made me remember the ice cream I had put in the refrigerator in the apartment, and I was deciding whether to go up and get it, when suddenly Arrow was there telling me to stand up. He grabbed my shoulder and yanked me up and told me to put up my hands and get set, and then he hauled off and socked me. I don't know how many times he hit me, but look at me. Finally they blocked him off and a cop came. I edged out, on out of the bar, and took an elevator up to the apartment, and Vince let me in. That part is a little hazy, but I know they put me on a couch because I woke up by falling off it, only I wasn't really awake. I had some kind of idea about being hurt and wanting to see the nurse, and I went to Bert's room and on in. The window curtains were drawn, and I turned on a light and went to the bed. He looked dead, with his mouth open, and I pulled the covers down and felt for his heart and he felt dead. There were two hot-water bags there, one on each side of him. They looked empty, and I picked one up and it *was* empty, and I thought to myself, she was careless because I made her sore and that won't do, and the other one was empty too, and I took them to the bathroom before I went—"

"Paul!" It was Louise, staring at him. "You told me you emptied them!"

"Sure I did." He grinned at her, or tried to. "I didn't want you to report her to the doctor. What the hell, can't a man be gallant?" He returned to Wolfe.

"You said I had to tell you something else. Okay, that's something else. Like it?"

"So you lied to Louise," Tuttle rumbled.

"Or you're lying now," David said, not tired at all. "You have said nothing about this to me."

"Of course not. Damn it, I was being gallant."

They all pitched in, cawing at one another, all in the family. With Louise's high soprano, Paul's baritone, Tuttle's rumble, and David's falsetto, it made quite a quartette.

Wolfe shut his eyes and tightened his lips, took it up to a point, and then crashed the sound barrier. "Jabber! Stop it, please." He picked on Paul. "You, sir, speak of gallantry. I didn't mention that Miss Goren was here with Doctor Buhl. She was, and she told me of your visits to her apartment and your phone calls, so we'll leave gallantry out, but there are two points at issue. First, the fact: did you find the bags empty, or did you empty them?"

"I found them empty. I told my sister—"

"I know what you told your sister, and the reason you give. Taking it that you found the bags empty, surely it is frivolous to offer that as an item for the police. Doctor Buhl told me that even if Miss Goren neglected to put hot water in them, which he doesn't believe, it would have had no appreciable effect on the patient, so it has no appreciable effect on me. That is the second point. But your conjecture that something was substituted for the morphine—that might indeed have an effect if you can give it any support. Can you?"

"I don't have to. Let the police see if they can."

"No. That won't do. A conjecture is well enough for private exploration, but using it to put a man under official suspicion of homicide is inadmissible. For example, it would not be a fatuous conjecture if I guessed that you, not knowing of the agreement between your brother and Mr. Arrow, and assuming that you would inherit a third of his fortune, killed him; but certainly I would not proceed—"

"You'd better not," Paul cut in. His mug was contorted again, trying to grin. "I did know about the agreement."

"Yes? Who told you?"

"I did," David said. "Bert told me, and I told Paul and Louise."

"You see?" Wolfe turned a hand over. "There goes my conjecture. If I were stubborn I could of course still cling to it, guessing that you had anticipated it and conspired to meet it, knowing that your dead brother can't testify, but that would be witless if I had no single fact in support." He shook his head at Paul. "I'm afraid you're trying to open fire without ammunition. But I have been engaged to investigate, so I won't scrimp it." He went to David. "I know how you feel about this, Mr. Fyfe, so I don't expect anything significant from you, but a few questions won't hurt. What do you know about the morphine?"

"Nothing. Nothing at all, except that Doctor Buhl told us he had left some with the nurse to be given to Bert after we left."

"Did you go in your brother's room after Doctor Buhl left?"

"Yes, we all did—Paul and Louise and Vincent and I. We told him the dinner was excellent and we were sorry he couldn't be with us at the theater."

"Where was Mr. Arrow?"

"I don't know. I believe he had said something about changing his shirt."

"Did he go in your brother's room after Doctor Buhl left?"

"I don't know." David shook his head. "I'm sure I don't know."

Wolfe grunted. "Not that that would indict him. How about later, when you returned from the theater? Did he go in your brother's room then?"

"I don't think so. If he did I didn't see him." David was frowning. "I told you about the situation. The nurse was very upset and said she had phoned Doctor Buhl to send a replacement. When she told us what had happened Arrow left—that is, he left the apartment. Then my sister and the nurse had some words, and my sister told the nurse to go, and after she went my sister phoned Doctor Buhl and told him she and her husband would stay until a replacement came. Shortly after that I went home. I live in Riverdale."

"But before leaving you went to your brother's room?"

"Yes."

"How was he then?"

"He was sound asleep, making some noise breathing, but he seemed all right. When Louise phoned Doctor Buhl he told her that Bert had had half a grain of morphine and would probably not wake before morning."

Wolfe's head moved. "Mrs. Tuttle. You have heard what your brothers have said. Have you any corrections or additions?"

She was having a little trouble. Her mouth was working and her hands, in her lap, were clasped tight. She met Wolfe's look but didn't reply, until suddenly she cried, "It's not my fault! No one is going to blame it on me!"

Wolfe made a face. "Why should they, madam?"

"Because they did about my father! Do you know about my father?"

"I know how he died. Your brother told me."

"Well, they blamed me then—everybody did! Because I was taking care of him and I slept and didn't go to his room and find the open windows! They even asked me if I put a drug in my chocolate so I would sleep! A twenty-four-year-old girl doesn't have to take drugs to sleep!"

"Now, my dear." Tuttle patted her shoulder. "That's all in the past, it's all forgotten. There were no open windows in Bert's room Saturday night."

"But I sent the nurse away." She was talking to Wolfe. "And I told Doctor Buhl I would be responsible, and I went to bed and went to sleep without even looking at the hot-water bags, and they were empty." She jerked her head around to her younger brother. "Tell the truth, Paul, the real truth. Were the bags empty?"

He patted her too. "Take it easy, Lou. Sure they were empty, on my word of honor as a Boy Scout, but that didn't kill him and I never said it did."

"No one's blaming you," Tuttle assured her. "As for your going to sleep, why shouldn't you? It was after one o'clock, and Doctor Buhl had said Bert would sleep all night. Believe me, my dear, you're making a mountain out of a molehill."

Her head went down and her hands came up to cover her face, and her shoulders began to tremble. To Wolfe a lady in distress is a female having a fit, and if she starts yowling he gets to his feet faster than seems practical for his bulk and makes for the door and the elevator. Louise wasn't yowling. He eyed her sharply and warily for a moment, decided she probably wouldn't go off, and went to her husband.

"About going to sleep, Mr. Tuttle, you said after one o'clock. That was after Paul had got you out of bed to let him in?"

"Yes." He had a soothing hand on his wife's arm. "It took a little time, hearing what Paul had to say and getting him settled on the couch. Then we took a look in Bert's room and found him asleep, and went to bed."

"Did you sleep right through until Paul woke you around six in the morning?"

"I think my wife did. She was tired out. She may have stirred a little, but I don't think she awoke. I went to the bathroom a couple of times, I usually do during the night, but except for that I slept until Paul called us. The second time I went and opened the door of Bert's room, and didn't hear anything, so I didn't go in. Why? Is this important?"

"Not especially." Wolfe darted a glance at Louise, alert to danger, and back at him. "I am thinking of Mr. Arrow and trying to cover all the possibilities. Of course he had a key to the apartment, and so might have entered during the night, performed an errand if he had one, and left again. Might he not?"

Tuttle considered. To watch him consider I had to make an effort to forget his shiny dome and concentrate on his features. It would have been simpler if his eyes and nose and mouth had been on top of his head. "Possibly," he conceded, "but I doubt it. I'm not a very sound sleeper and I think I would have heard him. And he would have had to go through the living room and Paul was there on the couch, but of course Paul was pretty well gone."

"I was *all* gone," Paul asserted. "He would have had to slug me again if he wanted me to notice him."

He looked at Wolfe. "It's an idea. What kind of an errand?"

"No special kind. I'm merely asking questions. —Mr. Tuttle, when did you next see Mr. Arrow?"

"That morning, Sunday morning, he came to the apartment around nine o'clock, just after Doctor Buhl arrived."

"Where had he been?"

"I don't know. I didn't ask him and he didn't say. It was—well, it was in the presence of death. He asked us a great many questions, some of them impertinent, I thought, but under those circumstances I made allowances."

Wolfe leaned back, closed his eyes, and lowered his chin. The brothers sat and looked at him. Tuttle turned to his wife, smoothing her shoulder and murmuring to her, and before long she uncovered her face and lifted her head. He got a nice clean handkerchief from his breast pocket, and she took it and dabbed around with it. There was no sign of any tear gullies down her cheeks.

Wolfe opened his eyes and moved them from left to right and back again. "I see no likely advantage," he pronounced, "in keeping you longer. I had hoped it would be possible to reach a decision this evening"— he leveled at Paul—"but your conjecture about the morphine merits a little inquiry—by me, that is, and of course discreet. It would be no service to expose you to an action for slander." His eyes went to David and back across to Tuttle. "By the way, I haven't mentioned that Doctor Buhl asked me to let you know that if Miss Goren is charged with negligence he will advise her to bring such an action, and he will support it. She maintains that before she left she put hot wa-

ter in the bags, and he believes her. You will hear
further from me, probably not later—"

The doorbell rang. When we have company in the
office Fritz usually answers it, but I had a hunch,
which I frequently do, and I got up and, passing behind the customers' chairs, reached the hall in time to
head Fritz off on his way to the front. The stoop light
was on, and through the panel I saw a stranger—a
square-shouldered specimen about my age and nearly
my size. Telling Fritz I'd take it, I went and opened
the door to the extent allowed by the chain of the bolt
and asked through the crack, "Can I help you?"

A soft drawly voice slipped through. "I guess so.
My name's Arrow. Johnny Arrow. I want to see Nero
Wolfe. If you open the door that'll help."

"Yeah, but I'll have to ask him. Hold it a minute." I
shut the door, got a piece of paper from my pocket
and wrote "Arrow" on it, returned to the office and
crossed to Wolfe's desk, and handed him the paper.
The visitors were out of their chairs, ready to leave.

Wolfe glanced at the paper. "Confound it," he
grumped. "I thought I was through for the day. But
perhaps I can—very well."

I will concede that I can be charged with negligence, since I knew what had happened Saturday
night in the Churchill bar, but I deny that it was in-
tentional. I have as much respect for the furniture in
the office as Wolfe has, or Fritz. I just didn't stop to
consider, as I went to the front door and let the uranium prince in and ushered him to the office and
stepped aside to observe expressions on faces. When,
the instant he caught sight of Paul Fyfe, Arrow went
for him, I was too far away and therefore one of the
yellow chairs got busted. The consolation was that I
saw a swell demonstration of how Paul had got his

jaw bruised on both sides. Arrow jabbed with his left, hard enough to rock him off balance, and then swung his right and sent him some six feet crashing onto the chair. As he was reaching to yank him up, presumably to attend to the other eye, I got there and put my arm around his neck from behind, and my knee in his back. Tuttle was there, trying to grab Arrow's sleeve. David was circling around, apparently with the notion of getting in between them, which is rotten tactics. Louise was making shrill noises.

"Okay," I told them, "just back off. I've got him locked." Arrow tried to wriggle, found that the only question was which would snap first, his neck or his back, and quit. Wolfe spoke, disgusted, saying they had better go. Paul had scrambled to his feet, and for a second I thought he was going to take a poke at Arrow while I held him, but David had his arm, pulling him away. Tuttle went to Louise and started her out, and David got Paul moving. At the door to the hall David turned to protest to Wolfe, "You shouldn't have let him in, you might have known." When they were all in the hall I unlocked Arrow and went to see them out, and as they crossed the threshold I wished them good night, but only David wished me one in return.

Back in the office Johnny Arrow was sitting in the red leather chair, working his head gingerly forward and back to check on his neck. I may have been a little thorough, but with a complete stranger how can you tell?

I sat with my back to my desk and took him in as an object with assorted points of interest. He was a uranium millionaire, the very newest kind. He was a chronic jaw-puncher, no matter where. He knew a good-looking nurse when he saw one, and acted accordingly. And he had been nominated as a candidate for the electric chair. Quite a character for one so young. He wasn't bad-looking himself, unless you insist on the kind they use for cigarette ads. His face and hands weren't as rough and weathered as I would have expected of a man who had spent five years in the wilderness pecking at rocks, but since finding Black Elbow he had had time to smooth up some.

He quit working his head and returned my regard with a stare of curiosity from brown eyes that had wrinkles at their corners from squinting for uranium. "That was quite a squeeze," he said in his soft drawl, no animosity. "I thought my neck was broken."

"It should have been," Wolfe told him severely. "Look at that chair."

"Oh, I'll pay for the chair." He got a big roll of lettuce from his pants pocket. "How much?"

"Mr. Goodwin will send you a bill." Wolfe was scowling. "My office is not an arena for gladiators. You came, I suppose, in response to the message we left for you?"

He shook his head. "I didn't get any message. If you sent it to the hotel, I haven't been there since morning. What did it say?"

"Just that I wanted to see you."

"I didn't get it." He lifted a hand to massage the

side of his neck. "I came because *I* wanted to see *you*." He emphasized a word by stretching it. "I wanted to see that Paul Fyfe too, but I didn't know he was here, that was just luck. I wanted to see him about a trick he tried to work on a friend of mine. You know about the hot-water bags."

Wolfe nodded. "And me?"

"I wanted to see you because I understand you're fixing it up that I killed my partner, Bert Fyfe." The brown eyes had narrowed a little. Evidently they squinted at other things besides uranium. "I wanted to ask if you needed any help."

Wolfe grunted. "Your information is faulty, Mr. Arrow. I have been hired to investigate and decide whether any of the circumstances of Mr. Fyfe's death warrant a police inquiry, and for that I do need help. There is no question of 'fixing it up,' as you put it. Of course your offer of help was ironic, but I do need it. Shall we proceed?"

Arrow laughed. No guffaws; just an easy little chuckle that went with the drawl. "That depends on how," he said. "Proceed how?"

"With an exchange of information. I need some, and you may want some. First, I assume that you got what you already have from Miss Goren. If I'm wrong, correct me. You must have talked with her since four o'clock this afternoon. No doubt she thought she was reporting events accurately, but if she gave you the impression that I'm after you with malign intent she was wrong. Do you care to tell me whether the information that brought you here came from Miss Goren?"

"Certainly it did. She had dinner with me. Doctor Buhl came to the restaurant for her to bring her here."

If I'm giving the impression that he was eager to co-operate with Wolfe I am wrong. He was merely bragging. He was jumping at the chance to tell somebody, anybody, that Miss Goren had let him buy her a dinner.

"Then," Wolfe said, "you should realize that her report was ex parte, though I don't say she deliberately colored it. I will say this, and will have it typed and sign it if you wish, that so far I have found no shred of evidence to inculpate you with regard to Bertram Fyfe's death. Let's get on to facts. What do you know about the hot-water bags? Not what any one has told you, not even Miss Goren, but what do you know from your own observation?"

"Nothing whatever. I never saw them."

"Or touched them?"

"Of course not. Why would I touch them?" The drawl never accelerated. "And if you're asking because that Paul Fyfe says he found them empty, what has that got to do with facts?"

"Possibly nothing. I'm not a gull. When did you last see Bertram Fyfe alive?"

"Saturday evening, just before we left to go to the theater. I went in just for a minute."

"Miss Goren was there with him?"

"Yes, of course."

"You didn't go in to see him when you returned from the theater?"

"No. Do you want to know why?"

"I already know. You found what Mr. David Fyfe calls a situation, and you went out again, abruptly. I have inferred that you went to look for Paul Fyfe. Is that correct?"

"Sure, and I found him. After what Miss Goren

told us I would have spent the night finding him, but I didn't have to. I found him down in the bar."

"And assaulted him."

"Sure I did. I wasn't looking for him to shine his shoes." The easy little chuckle rippled out, pleasant and peaceful. "I guess I ought to be glad a cop stepped in because I was pretty mad." He looked at me with friendly interest. "That was quite a squeeze you gave me."

"What then?" Wolfe asked. "I understand you didn't return to the apartment."

"I sure didn't. Another cop came, but I was still mad and I didn't want to be held, so they got mad. They put handcuffs on me and one of them took me to a station house and locked me up. I wouldn't tell them who it was I had hit or why I hit him, and I guess they were trying to find him to make a charge. Finally they let me use a phone, and I got someone to send a lawyer and he talked me out. I went to the apartment and found that Paul Fyfe there, and that Tuttle and his wife, and Bert was dead. That doctor was there too."

"Of course it was a shock to find him dead."

"Yes, it was. It wouldn't have been if I had killed him, is that it?" Johnny Arrow chuckled. "If you're really straight on this, if you're not trying to fix me up, let me tell you something, mister. Bert and I had been knocking around together for five years, some pretty rough going. We never starved to death, but we came close to it. Nobody ever combed our hair for us. When we found Black Elbow it took a lot of hard fast work to sew up the claims, and neither of us could have swung it alone. That was when we had a lawyer put our agreement in writing, so if something happened to one of us there wouldn't be some outsiders mixing in and making trouble. It had got so we liked to be together, even when we rubbed. That was why I came to New York with him when he asked me to. There was nothing in New York I wanted. We could handle all our business matters in Black Elbow and Montreal. I sure didn't come here with him to kill him."

Wolfe was regarding him steadily. "Then he didn't come to New York on business?"

"No, sir. He said it was a personal matter. After we got here he got in touch with his sister and brothers, and I had the idea something was eating him from away back. He went to Mount Kisco a few times and took me along. We rode all around the place in a Cadillac. We went to the house where he was born, and went all through it—there's an Italian family living there now. We went and had ice cream sodas at Tuttle's drugstore. We went to see a woman that ran a rooming house he had lived in once, but she had gone years ago. Just last week he found out she was living in Poughkeepsie, and we drove up there."

It took him quite a while to get that much out because he never speeded up. There was the advantage that he didn't have to stop for breath. "I seem to be talking a lot," he said, "but I'm talking about Bert. For five years I didn't do much talking except to him, and now I guess I want to talk *about* him."

He cocked his head to consider a moment, and then went on. "I wouldn't want to be fixed up, and I wouldn't want to fix anyone else up, but I guess that was too vague what I said about something eating Bert from away back. He told me a little about it when we were sitting under a rock one day up in Canada. He said if we really hit it he might go back home and attend to some unfinished business. Do you know how his father died and how he was tried for murder?"

Wolfe said he did.

"Well, he told me about it. He said he had never claimed his share of the inheritance because he didn't want any part of the mess he had run away from, and if you knew Bert that wouldn't surprise you. He said he had always kidded himself that he had rubbed it out and forgotten it, but now that it looked as if we might hit big he was thinking he might go back and look around. And that's what he did. If he had anyone in particular in mind he never told me, but I noticed a few things. When he told his family what he was doing he watched their faces. When he told them he was getting a complete transcript of the testimony at his trial for murder they didn't like it. When he told them he had been to see the woman that ran the rooming house they didn't like that either. It looked to me as if he was trying to give them an itch to scratch."

His eyes narrowed a little, showing crinkles. "But don't get the idea I'm trying to fix anybody up. The doctor says Bert died of pneumonia, and I guess he's a good doctor. I just didn't want to leave it vague about why Bert came to New York. Got any more questions?"

Wolfe shook his head. "Not at the moment. Later perhaps. But I suggested an exchange of information. Do you want any?"

"Now I call that polite." Arrow sounded as if he really appreciated it. "I guess not." He rose from the chair, and stood a moment. "Only you said you've found no evidence to—what was that word?"

"Inculpate."

"That's it. So why don't you just move out? That's

what Bert and I did when we found a field was dead, we moved out."

"I didn't say it was dead." Wolfe was glum. "It's not, and that's the devil of it. There is one mysterious circumstance that must somehow be explained before I can move out."

"What is it?"

"I've already asked you about it, and you dispute it. If I broach it again with you I'll be better armed. Mr. Goodwin will send you a bill for the chair when we know the amount. Good evening, sir."

He wanted more about the mysterious circumstance, but didn't get it. Nothing doing. When he found the field was dead he moved out, and I went to the hall to open the door for him. After he crossed the sill he turned to tell me, "That sure was a squeeze."

In the office, Wolfe was leaning back with his eyes closed, frowning. I stowed the broken chair in a corner, put the others back in place, straightened up my desk for the night, locked the safe, and then approached him. "What's the idea, trying to make him mad? If there's a mysterious circumstance I must have been asleep. Name it."

He muttered, without opening his eyes, "Hot-water bags."

I stretched and yawned. "I see. You force yourself to go to work, find there is no problem, and make one up. Forget it. Settle for the grand, which isn't too bad for eight hours' work, and vote no. Case closed."

"I can't. There is a problem." His eyes opened. "Who in the name of heaven emptied those bags, and why?"

"Paul did. Why not?"

"Because I don't believe it. Disregarding his repeated declarations here this evening, though they were persuasive, consider the scene. He enters his brother's room and finds him dead. He pulls the covers down and finds the hot-water bags empty. He turns to go and call his sister and brother-in-law, but it occurs to him that the empty bags are a weapon that may be used on Miss Goren. He doesn't want them to come to his sister's attention, so before he calls her he puts the bags in the bathroom. You accept that as credible?"

"Certainly I do, but—"

"If you please. I'll use the 'but.' But try it this way. He enters his brother's room and finds him dead. He pulls the covers down to feel the heart. The bags are there, with water in them. Seeing them, he conceives a stratagem—and remember, he is under the shock of just having found a corpse where he expected, presumably, to find his living brother. He conceives, on the spot, before calling the others, the notion of taking the bags to the bathroom and emptying them, so he can go at some future time to Miss Goren and tell her he found them empty; and he proceeds to do so. Do you accept that as credible?"

"It's a little fancy," I admitted, "as you describe it."

"I describe it as it must have happened, *if* it happened. I say it didn't. He noticed the bags only because they *were* empty; if they had been full he probably wouldn't have been aware of them at all, there in a sickbed, now a deathbed. Doubtless there are men capable of so sly an artifice at such a moment, but he is not one of them. I am compelled to assume that he found the bags empty, and where does that leave me?"

"I'd have to look it over." I sat down.

"You won't like it." He was bitter. "I don't. If I am

to preserve my self-esteem, a duty that cannot be delegated, I have got to explore it. Is Miss Goren at fault? Did she put the bags in the bed empty?"

"No, sir. I'm thinking of marrying her. Besides, I don't believe it. She's competent, and no competent trained nurse could possibly pull such a boner."

"I agree. Then here we are. Around midnight, just before she left, Miss Goren filled the bags with hot water and put them in the bed. Around six in the morning Paul Fyfe found the bags there in the bed, but they were empty. Someone had removed them, emptied them, and put them back. Justify it."

"Don't look at me, I didn't do it. Why should I justify it?"

"You can't. To suppose it was done with murderous design would be egregious. It's inexplicable; and anything inexplicable on a deathbed is sinister, especially the deathbed of a millionaire. Before I can even consider the question of who did it I must answer the question, why?"

"Not necessarily," I argued. "I'll switch. Settle for the grand, but don't vote no. Vote yes, and let Paul turn it over to the cops. That will fill the order."

"Pfui. Do you mean that?"

I gave up. "No. You're stuck. The cops would only decide the nurse had left the bags empty and wouldn't admit it, and Johnny Arrow would start in slugging the whole damn Homicide Squad from Inspector Cramer right down the line." Struck with a sudden suspicion, I eyed him. "Is this just a build-up? Do you already know why the bags were emptied, or think you do, and you want me to realize how brilliant you were to get it?"

"No. I am lost. I can't even grope. It's more than mysterious, it's preposterous." He looked up at the clock. "It's bedtime, and now I must take this monstrosity to bed with me. First, though, some instructions for you for the morning. Your notebook, please?"

I got it from the drawer.

## V

Wednesday morning, after having breakfast in the kitchen with Fritz, as usual, while Wolfe was having his up in his room, also as usual, I got started on the instructions. They were simple, but it proved to be not so simple to carry them out. The first and main item was to phone Doctor Buhl and arrange for him to be at the office at eleven o'clock, when Wolfe would come down from the plant rooms, and bring Anne Goren with him. To begin with, I didn't get hold of him until nearly noon. From nine o'clock until ten all I got was his answering service and the information that he was out making calls. I left word for him to ring me, but he didn't. From ten o'clock on I got his office nurse. She was courteous and sympathetic, in a subdued way, the first three times I phoned, but after that got a little brusque. The doctor, still out making the rounds, had been told of my request to be rung, and she couldn't help it if he had been too busy. When he finally called I couldn't very well ask him to arrive with Miss Goren at eleven, since it was already a quarter to twelve, so I suggested three o'clock, and got a flat no. Neither three nor any other hour. He had told Wolfe all he had to tell about the death of Bertram Fyfe, but if Wolfe wished to speak with him on the phone he could spare two minutes. Consulted, Wolfe said no, not on the phone. Deadlock.

The upshot was that after lunch I got the car from the garage and drove the forty miles, up the West Side Highway and out the Sawmill River Parkway, to Mount Kisco, and found that Buhl's office was in a big white house in a big green lawn. I had been told he would see me after his p.m. office hours, which were from two to four, but there were still five patients in the waiting room when I arrived, so I had a nice long visit with the usual crop of magazines before the nurse, who had been with him at least sixty years, passed me through.

Buhl, seated at a desk, looking tired but still distinguished, told me abruptly, "I have calls to make and I'm late. What is it now?"

I can be abrupt too. "A question," I said, "raised by a relative of the deceased. Did someone substitute something else for the morphine? Mr. Wolfe doesn't want to pass it on to the cops without giving it a look himself, but if you would prefer—"

"Morphine? You mean the morphine administered to Bert Fyfe?"

"Yes, sir. Since the question has been—"

"That damn fool. Paul, of course. It's absurd. Substituted when and by whom?"

"Not specified." I sat down, uninvited. "But Mr. Wolfe can't just skip it so he'd appreciate a little information. Did you give the morphine to the nurse yourself?"

From the look he gave me I expected to be told to go climb a tree, preferably one about ready to topple, but he changed his mind and decided to get it over with. "The morphine," he said, "came from a bottle in my case. I took two quarter-grain tablets from the bottle and gave them to the nurse, and told her to give one to the patient as soon as the dinner guests had left, and the other one an hour later if necessary. She has told me that the tablets were administered as directed. To suppose that something was substituted for them is fantastic."

"Yes, sir. Where did she keep them until the time came to administer them?"

"I don't know. She is a competent nurse and completely reliable. Do you want me to ask her?"

"No, thanks, I will. Could there be any question about your bottle of morphine? Could it have been tampered with?"

"Not possible. No."

"Had you got a fresh supply recently—I mean, put a fresh supply in that bottle?"

"No. Not for two weeks at least. Longer, probably."

"Would you say there is any chance—say one in a million—that you took the tablets from the wrong bottle?"

"No. Not one in a billion." His brows went up. "Isn't this a little superfluous? From what David told me yesterday I gathered that Paul's suspicions were directed at the man who came to New York with Bert —Mr. Arrow."

"Maybe so, but Mr. Wolfe is being thorough. He's a thorough man." I stood up. "Many thanks, doctor. If you wonder why I drove clear up here just for this, Mr. Wolfe is also careful. He doesn't like to ask questions about an unexpected death on the phone."

I left him, went back out to the car, and rolled off. The route back to the parkway took me through the center of town, and on a red brick building on a corner, a very fine location, I saw the sign: TUTTLE'S PHARMACY. That was as good a place as any for a phone, so I parked down the block and walked back to it. Inside,

it was quite an establishment—up-to-date, well-fur-
nished, well-stocked, and busy, with half a dozen customers on stools at the fountain and three or four
others scattered around. One of them, at a counter in
the rear, was being waited on by the proprietor himself, Vincent Tuttle. I crossed to a phone booth, dialed
the operator, asked for the number I knew best, and
in a moment had Wolfe's voice in my ear.

"From a booth," I told him, "in Tuttle's pharmacy
in Mount Kisco. Quoting Doctor Buhl, the idea of a
switch on the morphine is absurd and fantastic. As for
its source, he gave two quarter-grain tablets to the
nurse from his private stock. Do I proceed?"

"No." It was a growl, as always when he was interrupted in the plant rooms. "Or rather, yes, but first
some further inquiry in Mount Kisco. After you left I
considered the question of the hot-water bags, and I
may have hit on the answer—or I may not. At any
rate, it's worth trying. See Mr. Paul Fyfe and ask him
what happened to the ice cream. You will remember—"

"Yeah, he bought it at Schramm's, to take back to
Mount Kisco for a Sunday party, and took it to Bert's
apartment and put it in the refrigerator. You say you
want to know what happened to it?"

"I do. See him and ask him. If he accounts for it,
check him thoroughly. If he doesn't, see if Mr. or Mrs.
Tuttle can, and check them. If they can't, ask Miss
Goren when you see her about the morphine. If she
can't, find Mr. Arrow and ask him. I want to know
what happened to that ice cream."

"You certainly do. Tell me why so I'll have some
idea what I'm after."

"No. You are not without discretion, but there's no
point in subjecting it to an unnecessary strain."

"You're absolutely right, and I appreciate it deeply. Tuttle's right here, so shall I see him first?"

He said no, to see Paul first, and hung up. As I left the booth and the store and headed for the address of Paul's real-estate office, down the street a block, I was looking around inside my skull for a connection between Schramm's famous mango ice cream and the hot-water bags in Bert Fyfe's bed, but if it was there I couldn't find it. Which was just as well, if there really was one, because I hate to overwork my discretion.

I found Paul on the second floor of an old wooden building, above a grocery store. His office was one small room, with two desks and some scarred old chairs which had probably been allotted to him when the family split up the paternal estate. Seated at the smaller desk was a woman with a long thin neck and big ears, about twice Paul's age, who was perfectly safe even with him. Paul, at the other desk, didn't get up as I entered.

"You?" he said. "You got something?"

I looked at the woman, who was fiddling with some papers. He told her she could go, and she merely plunked a weight down on the papers, got up, and left. No amenities at all.

When the door had closed behind her I answered him. "I haven't got something, I'm just after something. Mr. Wolfe sent me up here to ask Doctor Buhl about the morphine and to ask you about the ice cream. The last we heard it was still in the refrigerator in your brother's apartment. What happened to it?"

"Well, for God's sake." He was staring at me, at least with his good eye. It was hard to tell what the one with the shiner was doing. "What the hell has that got to do with anything?"

"I don't know. With Mr. Wolfe, I often don't know, but it's his car and tires and gas, and he pays my salary, so I just humor him. It's the simplest and quickest way for you too, unless there's something about the ice cream you'd rather keep to yourself."

"There's not a damn thing about the ice cream."

"Then I won't have to bother to sit down. Did you bring it to Mount Kisco for the Sunday party you mentioned?"

"No. I didn't come back to Mount Kisco until Sunday night."

"But you were in New York again the next day, Monday, for the funeral—and to call on Miss Goren again. Did you get the ice cream then?"

"Look," he said, "we'll leave Miss Goren out of this."

"That's the spirit," I said warmly. "I'm all for gallantry. But what happened to the ice cream?"

"I don't know and don't give a damn."

"Did you see it or touch it at any time after you put it in the refrigerator Saturday afternoon?"

"I did not. And if you ask me, this is a lot of crap. I don't know where that fat slob Wolfe got his reputation, but if this is the way he carries on an investi— What's the big rush?"

I had got as far as the door. Turning as I opened it, I said politely, "Nice to see you," and went.

Backtracking to Tuttle's pharmacy, I found there had been a turnover of customers, but business was still humming. Tuttle's shiny dome loomed behind a showcase of cosmetics. Catching his eye, I crossed over and told him I would like to have a couple of minutes when he was free, and then went to the foun-

tain and ordered a glass of milk. It was nearly all
down when he called to me, and beckoned, and I emptied the glass and followed him to the rear, behind the
partition. He leaned against a counter and said it was
a surprise, seeing me up there.

"A couple of little errands," I told him. "To ask
Doctor Buhl about the morphine, and to ask you about
the ice cream. I've already asked Paul Fyfe. You remember he bought some ice cream at Schramm's Saturday afternoon and took it to Bert's apartment and
put it in the refrigerator, intending to take it home
with him."

Tuttle corrected me. "I remember he said he did.
What about it?"

"Mr. Wolfe wants to know what became of it. Paul
says he doesn't know. He says he never saw it again
after he put it in the refrigerator. Did you?"

"I never saw it at all."

"I thought you might have. You and your wife
stayed there Saturday night. Sunday morning your
brother-in-law was there dead, but even so you must
have eaten something. I thought you might have gone
to the refrigerator for something for breakfast, and
you might have noticed the ice cream."

"We had breakfast sent up." Tuttle was frowning.
"There was no equipment there for cooking. But now
that I think of it, I believe Paul mentioned the ice
cream Saturday evening at the dinner table. He said
something about my ice cream here not comparing
with Schramm's and asked why I didn't carry it, and I
told him Schramm's products were sold only at their
own stores, and anyway it was too expensive. Then I
believe my wife mentioned it on Sunday, when she
went to the refrigerator for some ice for drinks."

"Did you eat any of it Sunday? Or bring it home with you?"

"No. I said I never saw it. We stayed at the apartment until Monday and came home after the funeral."

"You don't know what became of it?"

"I do not. I suppose it's still there. Unless that man Arrow—why don't you ask him?"

"I will. But first, since I'm here, I guess I'll ask your wife. Is she around?"

"She's at home, up on Iron Hill Road. I can phone her and tell her you're coming, or you can speak with her on the phone. But I fail to see what that ice cream has to do with the death of my brother-in-law. What's the connection?"

It seemed to me that that reaction was rather late, but it could have been that since he was only an in-law he didn't want to butt in. "Search me," I told him. "I just run errands. Why don't we get your wife on the phone, and I may not have to bother her by going there?"

He turned to a phone on the counter, dialed a number, got it, told his wife I wanted to ask her something, and handed me the transmitter. Louise, not being an in-law, said at once that it was ridiculous to annoy them about something utterly irrelevant, but after a little give and take she told me what she knew, which was nothing. She had never seen the ice cream, though she had probably seen the package. Getting ice from the refrigerator Sunday afternoon, she had noticed a large paper bag on the bottom shelf, and, on returning to the living room, had mentioned it to her husband and her brother David, who was there, saying that she thought it was Paul's ice cream and asking if they wanted some. They had declined, and she had not looked into the paper bag. She had no idea what had happened to it. I thanked her, hung up, thanked her husband, and beat it.

Next stop, 48th Street, Manhattan.

## VI

In view of the parking situation, or rather the non-parking situation, I have given up using the car for midtown errands, so I left the highway at 46th Street and drove to the garage. I could have phoned a progress report to Wolfe from there, but the house is just around the corner, and I went in person instead of phoning, and got a surprise. In response to my ring it wasn't Fritz who unbolted the door for me, but Saul Panzer. Saul, with his big nose taking half the available area of his narrow little face, looks at first glance as if he might need help to add two and two. Actually he needs help for nothing whatever. He is not only the best of the four or five operatives Wolfe calls on as required, he's the best anywhere.

"So," I greeted him, "you got my job at last, huh? Please show me to the office."

"Got an appointment?" he demanded, closing the door. Then he followed me down the hall and in.

Wolfe, behind his desk, grunted at me. "Back so soon?"

"No, sir," I told him. "This is just a stopover after leaving the car at the garage. Do you want a report on Paul and Mr. and Mrs. Tuttle before I go on?"

"Yes. Verbatim, please."

With him verbatim means not only all the words but also all the actions and expressions, and I sat down and gave them to him. He is the best listener I know, usually with his elbow on the chair arm, his chin resting on his fist, and his eyes half closed.

When I had finished he sat a moment and then nodded. "Satisfactory. Proceed with the others. Since you won't need the car may Saul use it?"

That wasn't as chummy as it sounds. It had long been understood that the car was his one piece of property on which I had the say.

"For how long?" I inquired.

"Today, tonight, and possibly part of tomorrow."

I looked at my wrist and saw 6:55. "There's not much left of today. Okay. Do I ask for what?"

"Not at the moment. It may be to chase a wild goose. What about your dinner?"

"I don't know." I arose. "If I find the ice cream I can eat that." I headed for the door, turned there to suggest, "Saul can eat the goose," and left.

Flagging a taxi at Tenth Avenue and riding uptown, and across 48th Street to the East Side, a part of the thousand-wheeled worm, I admitted that he must have a glimmer of something, since Saul's daily rate was now fifty bucks, quite a bite out of a measly grand, but I still couldn't tie up the ice cream and the hot-water bags. Of course he might be sending Saul on a different trail entirely, and as far as keeping it to himself was concerned, I had long ago stopped letting that get on my nerves, so I just tabled it.

The number, on 48th between Lexington and Third, belonged to an old brick four-story that had been painted yellow. In the vestibule two names were squeezed on the little slip by the button next to the top—"Goren" and "Poletti." I pushed the button, and, when the clicks came, opened the door and entered, and went up two flights of narrow stairs, which were carpeted and clean for a change. Turning to the front on the landing, I got a surprise. A door had opened, and standing on the sill was one named neither Goren nor Poletti. It was Johnny Arrow, squinting at me.

"Oh," he said. "I thought maybe it was that Paul Fyfe."

I advanced. "If it's convenient," I said, "I'd like to see Miss Goren."

"What about?"

He needed taking down a peg. "Really," I said. "Only yesterday you were bragging about taking her to dinner. Don't tell me you've already been promoted to watchdog. I want to ask her a question."

For a second I thought he was going to demand to know the question, and so did he, but he decided to chuckle instead. He invited me in, ushered me through an arch into a living room that was well cluttered with the feminine touch, disappeared, and in a minute was back.

"She's changing," he informed me. He sat. "I guess you called me about bragging." His drawl was friendly. "We just got back from the ball game a little while ago, and now we're going out for a feed. I was going to phone you this morning."

"You mean phone Nero Wolfe?"

"No, you. I was going to ask you where you bought that suit you had on last night. Now I'd like to ask you where you bought the one you've got on now, but I guess that's a little personal."

I was sympathetic. Realizing that a guy who had spent five years in the bush, and who, in New York, found himself suddenly faced with the problem of togging up for a ladylove, was in a tough spot, especially if he could scrape up only ten million bucks, I gave him the lowdown from socks to shirts. We were on ornamental vests, pro and con, when Anne Goren

came floating in, and at sight of her I regretted the
steer I had given him. I would have been perfectly
willing to feed her myself if I hadn't been working.

"Sorry I made you wait," she told me politely.
"What is it?" She didn't sit, and we were up.

"A couple of little points," I said. "I saw Doctor
Buhl this afternoon, and expected he would phone
you, but since you were out he couldn't. First about
the morphine he gave you Saturday to be given to
Bertram Fyfe. He says he took two quarter-grain tablets from a bottle he had, and gave them to you, with
directions. Is that correct?"

"Wait a minute, Anne." Arrow was squinting at
me. "What's the idea of this?"

"No special idea." I met the brown eyes through
the squint. "Mr. Wolfe needs the information to clear
this thing up, that's all.—Do you object to giving it,
Miss Goren? I asked Doctor Buhl where you kept the
tablets until the time came to administer them, and he
told me to ask you."

"I put them in a saucer and put the saucer on top
of the bureau in the patient's room. That is standard
procedure."

"Sure. Would you mind going right through it?
From the time Doctor Buhl gave you the tablets?"

"He handed them to me just before he left, and
after he left I went to the bureau and put them in the
saucer. The instructions were to give one as soon as
the guests had gone, and one an hour later if it
seemed desirable, and that's what I did." She was being cool and professional. "At ten minutes past eight I
put one of the tablets in my hypo syringe with one c.c.
of sterile water, and injected it in the patient's arm.
An hour later he was asleep but a little restless, and I

did the same with the other tablet. That quieted him completely."

"Have you any reason to suspect that the tablets in the saucer had been changed by someone? That the ones you gave the patient were not the ones Doctor Buhl gave you?"

"Certainly not."

"Look here," Johnny Arrow drawled, "that's a kind of a nasty question. I guess that's enough."

I grinned at him. "You're too touchy. If the cops ever got started on this they'd hammer away at her for hours. Five people have admitted they were in the patient's room after Doctor Buhl left, including you, and the cops would go over that with her forward, backward, sideways, and up and down. I don't want to spoil her appetite for dinner, so I merely ask her if she saw anything suspicious. Or heard anything. You didn't, Miss Goren?"

"I did not."

"Then that's that. Now the other point. You may or may not know that Paul Fyfe brought some ice cream to the apartment and put it in the refrigerator. It was mentioned at the dinner table, but you weren't there. Do you know what happened to the ice cream?"

"No." Her voice sharpened. "This seems pretty silly. Ice cream?"

"I often seem silly. Just ignore it. Mr. Wolfe wants to know about the ice cream. You know nothing at all about it?"

"No. I never heard of it."

"Okay." I turned to Arrow. "This one is for you too. What do you know about the ice cream?"

"Nothing." He chuckled. "You can get as nasty as you want to with me, after that squeeze you put on

me last night, but don't try getting behind me. I'm
going to keep you right in front."

"From the front I use something else. You remember Paul Fyfe mentioned the ice cream at the dinner
table?"

"I guess I do. I had forgotten about it."

"But you never saw it or touched it?"

"No."

"Or heard anything about what happened to it?"

"No."

"Then I'm going to ask you to do me a favor. You'll
be doing yourself one too, because it's the quickest
way to get rid of me. Where are you going for dinner?"

"I've got a table reserved at Rusterman's."

He was certainly learning his way around, possibly with Anne's help. "That's fine," I said, "because
it's only a block out of the way. I want you to take me
to the Churchill Towers apartment and let me look in
the refrigerator."

It was a good thing I had taken the trouble to brief
him on tailors and haberdashers. But for that he
would probably have refused, and I would have had to
go and persuade Tim Evarts, the house dick, to oblige,
and that would have cost both time and money. He
did balk some, but Anne put in, saying it would take
less time to humor me than to argue with me, and
that settled it. It seemed likely that in the years to
come Anne would do a lot of settling, and then and
there I decided to let him have her. She permitted
him to help her get a yellow embroidered stole across
her bare shoulders, and he got a black Homburg from
a table. On our way downstairs, and in the taxi we
took to the Churchill, I could have coached him on

black Homburgs, when and where and with what, but with Anne present I thought it advisable to skip it.

The Churchill Towers apartment, on the thirty-second floor, had a foyer about the size of my bedroom, and the living room would have accommodated three billiard tables with plenty of elbow space. There was an inside hall between the living room and the bedrooms, and at one end of the hall was a serving pantry, with an outside service entrance. Besides a long built-in stainless-steel counter, the pantry had a large warmer cabinet, an even larger refrigerator, and a door to a refuse-disposal chute, but no cooking equipment. Arrow and Anne stood just inside the swinging door, touching elbows, as I went and opened the door of the refrigerator.

The freezing compartment at the top held six trays of ice cubes and nothing else. On the shelves below were a couple of dozen bottles—beer, club soda, tonic—five bottles of champagne lying on their sides, a bowl of oranges, and a plate of grapes. There was no paper bag, big or little, and absolutely no sign of ice cream. I closed the door and opened the door of the warmer cabinet. It contained nothing. I opened the door of the disposal chute and stuck my head in, and got a smell, but not of ice cream.

I turned to the hooker and the hooked. "All right," I told them, "I give up. Many thanks. As I said, this was the quickest way to get rid of me. Enjoy your dinner." They made gangway for me, and I pushed through the swinging door and on out.

When Wolfe had asked me what about dinner I had told him I didn't know, but I knew now. I could be home by 8:30, and that afternoon, preparing for one of Wolfe's favorite hot-weather meals, Fritz had been collecting eight baby lobsters, eight avocados, and a bushel of young leaf lettuce. When he had introduced to them the proper amounts of chives, onion, parsley, tomato paste, mayonnaise, salt, pepper, paprika, pimientos, and dry white wine, he would have Brazilian lobster salad as edited by Wolfe, and not even Wolfe could have it all stowed away by half past eight.

He hadn't. I found him in the dining room, at table, starting on deep-dish blueberry pie smothered with whipped cream. There was no lobster salad in sight, but Fritz, who had let me in, soon entered with the big silver platter, and there was plenty left. Wolfe's ban on business during meals is not only for his own protection but other people's too, including me, so I could keep my mind where it belonged, on the proper ratio of the ingredients of a mouthful. Only after that had been attended to, and my share of the blueberry pie, and we had crossed the hall to the office, where Fritz brought coffee, did he ask for a report. I gave it to him. When I had described the climax, the empty refrigerator—that is, empty of ice cream—I got up to refill our coffee cups.

"But," I said, "if you have simply got to know what happened to it, God knows why, there is still one slender hope. David wasn't on my list. I was going to phone from the Churchill to ask if you wanted me to try him, but I wanted some of that lobster. He was there in the apartment most of Sunday. Shall I see him?"

Wolfe grunted. "I phoned him this afternoon, and he was here at six o'clock. He says he knows nothing about it."

"Then that's the crop." I sat and took a sip of coffee. Fritz' coffee is the best on earth. I've done it exactly as he does, but it's not the same. I took another sip. "So the gag didn't work."

"It is not a gag."

"Then what is it?"

"It is a window for death. I think it is—or was. I'll leave it at that for tonight. We'll see tomorrow, Archie."

"Yes, sir."

"I don't like the slant of your eye. If you're thinking of badgering me, don't. Go somewhere."

"Glad to. I'll go have another piece of pie." I took my cup and saucer and headed for the kitchen.

I spent the rest of the evening there, chewing the rag with Fritz, until his bedtime came, eleven o'clock, and then went to the office to lock the safe and tell Wolfe good night, and mounted the two flights to my room. I have been known to feel fairly well satisfied with myself as I got ready for bed after a day's work, but not that night. I had failed to learn the fate of the ice cream. I hadn't the faintest notion where the ice cream came in. I didn't know what a window for death was, though I knew what it had been on a winter night twenty years ago. One of the noblest functions of a man is to keep millionaires from copping pretty girls, and I hadn't moved a finger to stop Arrow. And the case was no damn good anyhow, with a slim chance of getting any more out of it than the thousand bucks, and with the job limited to deciding whether to call the cops in or not. It was a bad setup all the way. Usually I'm asleep ten seconds after I hit the pillow, but that night I tossed and turned for a full minute before I went off.

The trouble with mornings is that they come when you're not awake. It's all a blur until I am washed and dressed and have somehow made my way down to the kitchen, and got orange juice in me, and I'm not really awake until the fourth griddle cake and the second cup of coffee. But that Thursday morning it was accelerated. As I picked up the glass of orange juice I became aware through the blur that Fritz was putting stuff on a tray, and glanced at my wrist.

"My God," I said, "you're late. It's a quarter past eight."

"Oh," he said, "Mr. Wolfe already has his. This is for Saul. He's up with Mr. Wolfe. He said he already had breakfast, but you know how he likes my summer sausage."

"When did he come?"

"About eight o'clock. Mr. Wolfe wants you to go up when you're through breakfast." He picked up the tray and went.

That did it. I was awake. But that was no good either, because it kept me from enjoying my breakfast. I ate the sausage all right, but forgot to taste it, and I also forgot to put honey on the last cake until it was half gone. I had the *Times* propped on the rack in front of me, and pretended to read it, but didn't. It was only 8:32 when I took the last gulp of coffee, shoved my chair back, went to the hall and up one flight to Wolfe's room, found the door open, and entered.

Wolfe, in his yellow pajamas and barefooted, was seated at the table near a window, and Saul, chewing on griddle cake and sausage, was across from him. I approached.

"Good morning," I said coldly. "Shoe shine?"

"Archie," Wolfe said.

"Yes, sir. Suit pressed?"

"This is no time of day for you, I know, but I want to get on with this. Get all of them, including Doctor Buhl. Arrange for them to be here at eleven o'clock, or if that's impossible, at noon. Tell them I have made my decision and wish to communicate it. If Doctor Buhl is obstinate, tell him that the decision, and my reasons for it, will be of considerable professional interest to him, and that I feel strongly he should be present. If you phone him immediately you may get him before he starts his day's work. Get him first."

"Is that all?"

"For the present, yes. I need a little more time with Saul."

I left them.


# VII

It was twenty minutes to twelve when, after a buzz from me on the house phone to tell him they were all there, Wolfe entered, crossed to his desk, greeted them with a nod to the left and one to the right, and sat. On the phone Doctor Buhl and I, after a warm discussion, had settled for eleven-thirty, but he was ten minutes late.

I had given David, as the senior member of the family, the red leather chair. Doctor Buhl and Paul and the Tuttles were ranged in front of Wolfe's desk, with Paul next to me. I wanted him handy in case Johnny Arrow got a notion to try another one-two on him. Arrow and Anne were in the rear, side by side, behind Doctor Buhl. Saul Panzer was over by the big globe, in one of the yellow chairs, with his feet, on their toes, pulled back. He always sits like that, even when we're playing pinochle.

Wolfe focused on David. "I was hired," he said, "to inquire into your brother's death and decide whether the police should be asked to investigate. I have decided in the affirmative. It is indeed a case for the police."

They made noises and exchanged glances. Paul turned his head to glare at Johnny Arrow. Louise Tuttle reached for her husband's arm. Doctor Buhl said with authority, "I challenge that decision. As the attending physician, I demand your reasons for it."

Wolfe nodded. "Of course, doctor. You are right to make that demand. Naturally the police will want my reasons too, as will the others here, and the simplest way to handle it is for me to dictate my memorandum to Inspector Cramer of the Homicide Squad in your presence." His eyes moved. "It will go better if none of you interrupt. If there are questions after I finish I'll answer them. Archie, your notebook, please. First a letter to Mr. Cramer."

I swiveled to get the notebook and pen, swiveled back, crossed my legs, and rested the notebook on my knee. That way I was facing the audience. "Shoot," I told him.

"Dear Mr. Cramer. I believe you should give your attention to the death of a man named Bertram Fyfe last Saturday night in his apartment at Churchill Towers. In support of that belief I enclose summaries of recent conversations with seven persons, with identifying data, and also a memorandum of the results of the inquiry I have made. Sincerely."

He wiggled a finger at me. "You will prepare the summaries and data, and the memorandum will tell you what should be included and what may be omitted. Start the memorandum on my letterhead, in the usual form. Understood?"

"Right."

He leaned back and took a breath. "The memorandum: Since three of the persons involved, including the deceased, are named Fyfe, I shall use first names. Paul's conjecture regarding the morphine can, I think, be ignored. To suppose that one of those present brought with him lethal tablets of some sort, so similar in appearance to the morphine tablets that they could be substituted without arousing the suspicion of the nurse, would be extravagant indeed. One person, Tuttle, the pharmacist, might have had such tablets or been able to get them or make them, but even so it would have to be assumed that he anticipated an opportunity to substitute them unobserved, also an extravagant assumption."

"It's ridiculous," Dr. Buhl declared. "Any lethal substance in the Pharmacopoeia would have left evidence that I would have detected."

"I doubt that, doctor. It's an overstatement, and I wouldn't advise you to repeat it on the witness stand. I asked you not to interrupt. Archie?"

He wanted the last three words, and I obliged. " 'An extravagant assumption.' "

"Yes. Therefore, after routine inquiry by Mr. Goodwin, I dismissed jugglery with the morphine as a mere chimera of Paul's spiteful fancy; and indeed I would have dismissed the whole matter on that basis but for one pesky thorn, the hot-water bags. Paragraph.

"I felt compelled to assume, and I am confident you would have agreed in the circumstances, that Paul had found the hot-water bags empty in the bed. That stumped me. After the departure of the nurse, sometime during the night, someone had taken the bags from the bed, emptied them, and put them back. For what conceivable reason? That could not be simply dismissed. I worried it. I sent Mr. Goodwin to Mount Kisco to inquire about the morphine, but that was mere routine. The empty hot-water bags had somehow to be explained. I considered them in every possible light, in relation to everything I had been told by all those concerned, and it came to me from two directions at once. The first was as a possible answer to the question, what purpose could empty bags serve in a bed better than full bags? The second was the fact that the Fyfes' father had also died of pneumonia, after someone had opened a window and let the winter cold in to him. A window of death. The question and the fact together brought me an idea. Paragraph.

"I made three phone calls—no, four. I phoned the manager of Schramm's store on Madison Avenue, and asked him how he packs two quarts of ice cream on a hot summer afternoon for a customer who wishes to take it some distance in a car. He said the ice cream is put in a cardboard container, and the container is put in a carton on a bed of dry ice, and chunks of dry ice are packed on both sides of it and on top. He said that is their invariable custom. I phoned Doctor Vollmer, who lives on this street, and at his suggestion I phoned an official of a firm which makes dry ice, and learned (a) that several pounds of chunks of dry ice, placed under the covering of a pneumonia patient near his chest, would certainly lower his temperature materially and probably dangerously; (b) that only a controlled experiment could tell how dangerously, but it might be fatal; (c) that if the dry ice pressed against the body, even with fabric between, it would burn the skin seriously and leave vivid marks; and (d) that a rubber bag would be perfect, between the ice and the body, for prevention of the burning. My fourth—"

"This is fantastic," Doctor Buhl said. "Perfectly fantastic."

"I agree," Wolfe told him. "I had something fantastic to account for. Paragraph. My fourth phone call was to David Fyfe, to ask him to come to see me. The next thing was to learn what had happened to the ice cream. The hypothesis I was forming was bootless if there was evidence that the package had been intact on Sunday, and when Mr. Goodwin phoned from Mount Kisco I asked him to inquire. He did so, of Paul, Mr. and Mrs. Tuttle, Miss Goren, and Mr. Arrow, and they all disclaimed any knowledge of it. He also—"

Louise Tuttle's high thin voice cut in. "That's not true! I told him I saw it in the refrigerator Sunday!"

Wolfe shook his head. "You told him you saw a large paper bag and supposed it contained the ice cream. You didn't look inside the bag. You didn't see the dry ice." His eyes were holding hers. "Did you?"

"Don't answer that," Tuttle said abruptly.

"Indeed." Wolfe's brows went up. "Have we reached a point where questions can't be answered? Did you look inside the bag, Mrs. Tuttle?"

"No! I didn't!"

"Then I'll proceed. Archie?"

I cued him. " 'it. He also.' "

"Yes. He also went to the apartment and looked in the refrigerator, and there was no sign of the ice cream. I had myself asked David, and he too had said he knew nothing about it. So my hypothesis now had some flesh and bone. Someone had done something with the ice cream and was lying about it. If the dry ice had been used in the manner suggested, to kill a pneumonia patient, it could never be proven, since dry ice leaves no trace whatever, and my assumption would have to remain an assumption. I had to tackle the problem from another direction, and in fact I had already prepared to do so by asking certain questions of David Fyfe and by sending for Saul Panzer. You know Saul Panzer. Paragraph.

"There had been a few intimations, as you will find in the enclosed summaries of conversations. Bert Fyfe had been tried for the murder of his father and acquitted. He had resented the testimony of his sister and brothers at the trial, and a major item in his defense was an alibi supplied by his friend Vincent Tuttle, who testified that they had been playing cards at the rooming house where they both had rooms. According to Mr. Arrow, Bert had come to New York not on business but, in Arrow's words, because something was eating him from away back. Arrow himself was of course not a target for suspicion, since he spent Saturday night in a police station. And other points you will not miss—the most suggestive being, I think, that Bert not only went to see the landlady he had rented a room from twenty years ago, but when he found she had gone to Poughkeepsie he went there to see her. As you will find from the summary of my conversation with David yesterday afternoon—I'll have to give you that, Archie—Bert had lived in her rooming house only a short time, about two months, hardly a sufficient period to form a bond so strong that after an absence of twenty years he would seek her out so persistently. It was a fair inference that he had some special purpose in mind. Paragraph.

"Other suggestive bits came from David yesterday afternoon in response to questions. His father's relations with his progeny, after the mother's death, had not been cordial. He had ordered Bert to leave and not return. He had been difficult with David and Paul. He had refused permission for his daughter to marry the young man named Vincent Tuttle, then a clerk in the local drugstore, and had commanded her not to see him. After his death Louise had married Tuttle, and later they had bought the drugstore with her share of the inheritance. I had known, of course, from a previous conversation, that the estate had been divided equally among the children."

Wolfe turned his head. "Before I go on, Mr. Tuttle, you might like to answer a question or two. Is it true that in your hearing, the day before he was taken ill, Bert mentioned the fact that he had seen Mrs. Dobbs, his and your former landlady, and talked with her?"

Tuttle passed his tongue over his lips. "I don't think so," he rumbled. He cleared his throat. "Not that I remember."

"Of course he did, Vince," David declared. He looked at Wolfe. "I told you yesterday."

"I know. I'm testing his memory." He went to Paul. "Do you remember it?"

"Yes." Paul's eyes were on Tuttle. "You're damn right I remember it. He said he was going to see her again as soon as he got well."

Wolfe grunted. "I won't ask you, Mrs. Tuttle." He focused on her husband again. "The other question. Where were you yesterday evening from six to ten o'clock?"

It floored him completely. He hadn't expected it and wasn't prepared for it. "Yesterday evening?" he asked lamely.

"Yes. From six to ten. To refresh your memory, Mr. Goodwin came to your store to ask you and your wife about the ice cream, and left around five-thirty."

"There's nothing wrong with my memory," Tuttle asserted. "But I don't have to submit to this. I don't have to account to you for my actions."

"Then you decline to answer?"

"You have no right to ask. It's none of your business."

"Very well. I merely thought you had a right to tell me. Archie?"

Since it had been a long interruption I gave him more than three words. I looked at my notebook. " 'That the estate had been divided equally among the children.' "

Wolfe nodded. "Paragraph. As you will see in the summary of my conversation with Mr. Arrow, he had told me that Bert had told his relatives that he had gone to see his former landlady; and David verified that yesterday evening and gave me the landlady's name—Mrs. Robert Dobbs. That has just been corroborated by Paul, as I dictate this. Clearly it was desirable to learn what Bert had wanted of Mrs. Dobbs, and since Mr. Goodwin might be needed for other errands I phoned Saul Panzer and had him come, and sent him to Poughkeepsie. David hadn't known her address, and it took Mr. Panzer a while to locate her. It was nearly ten o'clock when he got to the house where she lives with her married daughter. As he approached the door it opened and a man emerged, and as they met the man stopped him and asked whom he wanted to see. As you know, Mr. Panzer is highly sensitized and extremely discreet. He replied that he was calling on Jim Heaton, having learned the name of Mrs. Dobbs' son-in-law during his inquiries, and the man went on his way. Reporting to me later, Mr. Panzer described him, and the description fitted Vincent Tuttle. They are both in my office now, and Mr. Panzer identifies Mr. Tuttle as the man he saw emerging from that house last night."

Wolfe turned. "Saul?"

"Yes, sir. Positive."

"Mr. Tuttle, do you wish to comment?"

"No."

"That is wise, I think." He returned to me. "Paragraph. Before dictating the preceding paragraph I asked Mr. Tuttle where he was last evening, and he refused to tell me. I am also enclosing a summary of Mr. Panzer's conversation with Mrs. Dobbs. I must confess it is far from conclusive. She would not identify the man who had just left the house. She would not divulge the purpose of Bert Fyfe's visit to her. She would not discuss in any detail the events on that winter night twenty years ago. There are, of course, obvious conjectures. Was the alibi which Tuttle gave Bert a fraud, and Bert didn't dare to impeach it? Does Mrs. Dobbs know it was a fraud? Did Tuttle leave the rooming house that stormy night, but Bert didn't, and Mrs. Dobbs knows it? Did Tuttle go to the Fyfe home, and get admitted by Louise, and drug her chocolate drink, and later return and open the windows from the outside? I do not charge him with those acts, but the questions put themselves. I was not hired to find evidence to convict a murderer, but merely to decide whether a police investigation is called for, and I think it is, for the reasons given. I telephoned you this morning to suggest that you ask the Poughkeepsie police to put a guard on Mrs. Dobbs and the house she lives in, and said I would shortly tell you why. I have now told you. Paragraph.

"Many questions also put themselves regarding the death of Bert Fyfe. Merely as one example, if it is to be assumed that Vincent Tuttle, fearing exposure of a former crime, again undertook to help pneumonia kill a man, this time using dry ice instead of an open window, why did he leave the paper bag in the refrigerator that night, presumably with the ice cream still in it? Answer it as you will, failing an answer from him, but perhaps he did not know there was a disposal chute in the pantry; and when, on Sunday afternoon, he found that there was one, he took the first opportunity to dump the thing. As for the dry ice, it leaves no trace, so there is no record for you, but experts can furnish you with presumptions, as they did me. The chunks of ice were of course not put inside the bags; the limp empty bags were merely used as insulation to keep the ice from contact with the body. Probably the experts can tell you how long it would take small chunks of dry ice to wholly vaporize, but that point is not vital, since Mr. Tuttle was there in the apartment and could easily have had opportunity to remove the residue, if any, before Paul discovered the body. That, and other pertinent questions, I leave to you. I have done the job I was hired for, and I trust you will not find it necessary to consult me at any length. All the information I have goes to you with this."

Wolfe flattened his palms on the chair arms and took in the audience. "There it is," he said. "I didn't want to tell you about it and go all over it again for Mr. Cramer. Any questions?"

David was slumped in the red leather chair, his head down, staring at the floor. At Wolfe's question he slowly lifted his head and slowly moved it, taking in the others, one by one, and then going to Wolfe. He squeezed words out.

"I suppose I ought to feel sorry, but I don't. I always thought Bert killed his father. I always thought Vince's alibi was false, that he lied to save Bert, but I see it now. Without it Bert would probably have been convicted, so it did save him, but it saved Vince too. Of course Bert knew it was false, he knew he and Vince hadn't been together all evening, but if he said so, if he said Vince had gone out for a while, that would have destroyed his own alibi, and he didn't dare —and he didn't know Vince had killed our father. He might have suspected, but he didn't know. I see it now. I even see the Mrs. Dobbs part." He frowned. "I'm trying to remember her testimony. She said she hadn't heard either of them go out, but probably she had, and she might have known which one, but if she said she heard either of them leave the house that would have ruined Bert's alibi, and she was crazy about Bert and she hadn't liked our father. Not many people liked our father."

He thought he was going to say more, decided not to, rose from the chair, and turned to his brother. "Was this what you were after, Paul? Did you suspect this?"

"Hell no," Paul said harshly. "You know damn well what I suspected, and who, and if this fat slob is right about the dry ice"—he bounced out of his chair and wheeled to face Johnny Arrow—"why couldn't it have been him? He had a key to the apartment! I never said I knew exactly how he did it! And if you—now lay off!"

David had stepped across and grabbed his arm, and for a second I thought Paul was going to sock his elder brother, but evidently David knew him better than I did. David said nothing, but he didn't have to. He merely hung onto his arm, steered him around back of the other chairs, and headed him towards the hall. They disappeared, and Saul went to let them out.

"I have no questions," Doctor Buhl said. He arose and looked down at the Tuttles, then at Wolfe. "My God, after twenty years. You used a phrase, 'a window for death.' You have certainly opened one." He looked down again. "Louise, you have been my patient nearly all your life. Do you need me? Are you all right?"

"I'm all right." Her high thin voice was trying not to be a wail. "I don't believe it."

Buhl opened his mouth to say more, decided not to, and turned and went. Wolfe spoke to the man and wife who owned a fine drugstore. "If you have no questions you might as well go."

Louise, with her teeth bearing down on her lip, tugged at her husband's sleeve. He took a deep breath, put a hand on her shoulder, and raised himself from the chair, and she came up with him. Side by side they headed for the door, and I left them to Saul too. When they were out of sight Wolfe sent his eyes in the direction of the pair in the rear and said sharply, "Well? Have I fixed it up for you?"

Damned if they weren't holding hands, and they continued to hold as they got up and approached the desk. I am perfectly capable of holding hands, but not in public. Anne looked as if she wanted to cry but didn't intend to. Luckily it was Johnny's left hand she had, for he wanted to use the other one. When they got to the desk he stretched his arm across it and said, "Shake."

## VIII

I should explain one thing. Since Johnny and Anne had no part in the performance, why did Wolfe tell me to invite them? I didn't have to ask him. I know him. One little grand is a pretty skimpy fee for a job like that, spotting a murderer, and if Johnny Arrow came and saw the neat process by which the guy who had killed his partner was dug out he might feel inclined to show his appreciation by contributing a small hunk of uranium. That was the idea, no question about it, and for some weeks, as I flipped through the morning mail, I had my eye out for an envelope with his return address. It never came, and I quit expecting it.

But last week, just four days after a jury had convicted Vincent Tuttle of the first-degree murder of Bertram Fyfe's father—it had been decided to try him for that one because it was a tighter case, especially after Mrs. Dobbs opened up—here came an envelope with Fyfe-Arrow Mining Corporation, Montreal, in the corner, and when I opened it and saw the amount of the check I raised my brows as high as they would go. A really nice hunk.

There was no letter, but that was understandable. He had no time for writing letters. He was much too busy showing his wife how to prospect.

# Immune
## to Murder

# I

I stood with my arms folded, glaring down at Nero Wolfe, who had his 278 pounds planted in a massive armchair which was made of heavy pine slats, with thick rainbow rugs draped over the back and on the seat for a cushion. It went with the rest of the furniture, including the bed, in that room of River Bend, the sixteen-room mountain lodge belonging to O. V. Bragan, the oil tycoon.

"A fine way to serve your country," I told him. "Not. In spite of a late start I get you here in time to be shown to your room and unpack and wash up for dinner, and now you tell me to go tell your host you want dinner in your room. Nothing doing. I decline."

He was glaring back. "Confound it, I have lumbago!" he roared.

"You have not got lumbago. Naturally your back's tired, since all the way from Thirty-fifth Street, Manhattan, to the Adirondacks, three hundred and twenty-eight miles, you kept stiff on the back seat, ready to jump, even with me at the wheel. What you need is exercise, like a good long walk to the dining room."

"I say it's lumbago."

"No. It's acute mooditis, which is a medical term for an inflamed whim." I unfolded my arms to gesture. "Here's the situation. We were getting nowhere on that insurance case for Lamb and McCullough, which I admit was a little annoying for the greatest detective alive, and you were plenty annoyed, when a phone call came from the State Department. A new ambassador from a foreign country with which our country wanted to make a deal had been asked if he had any special personal desires, and he had said yes, he wanted to catch an American brook trout, and, what was more, he wanted it cooked fresh from the brook by Nero Wolfe. Would you be willing to oblige? Arrangements had been made for the ambassador and a small party to spend a week at a lodge in the Adirondacks, with three miles of private trout water on the Crooked River. If a week was too much for you, two days would do, or even one, or even in a pinch just long enough to cook some trout."

I gestured again. "Okay. You asked me what I thought. I said we had to stay on the Lamb and McCullough job. You said our country wanted that ambassador softened up and you must answer our country's call to duty. I said nuts. I said if you wanted to cook for our country you could enlist in the Army and work your way up to mess sergeant, but I would admit that the Lamb and McCullough thing was probably too tough for you. Days passed. It got tougher. The outcome was that we left the house at eleven-fourteen this morning and I drove three hundred and twenty-eight miles in a little under seven hours, and here we are. The setup is marvelous and very democratic. You're just here as a cook, and look at this room you've got." I swept a hand around. "Not a hardship in sight. Private bath. Mine is somewhat smaller, but I'm only cook's assistant, I suppose I might call it culinary attaché. We were told dinner at six-thirty because they have to get up early to go fishing, and it is now six-thirty-four, and I am instructed to go tell Bragan you'll eat in your room. Where would that leave me? They wouldn't want me at the table without you, and when will I get another chance to watch an ambassador eat? If you've got lumbago it's not in your back, it's in your psyche. It is called psychic lumbago. The best treatment—"

"Archie. Stop gibbering. 'Lumbago' denotes locality. From the Latin *lumbus*, meaning 'loin.' The psyche is not in the loin."

"No? Prove it. I'll concede that yours may not be, but I have known cases—for example, remember that guy, I forget his name, that wanted to hire you to arrange a meeting of his first four wives and persuade them—"

"Shut up!" He put his hands on the chair arms.

"Yes, sir."

"There are degrees of discomfort, and some of them stop short of torment, thank heaven. Very well." He levered himself upright, making some faces, assorted, on the way. "It is lumbago. And with it I am to sit at a strange table with a jumble of strangers. Are you coming?"

He headed for the door.


II


There was a hardship after all; the lodge had no dining room. Or maybe it did; but the assorted heads of deer and bear and moose on the walls, with planked fish here and there, made it also a trophy room; the billiard table at one end made it a game room; the cabinets of weapons and rods made it a gun-and-tackle room; the chairs and rugs and scattered tables with lights made it a living room; and the over-all size made it a barn.

There was nothing wrong with the food, which was served by two male experts in uniform, but I damn near roasted. There were nine of us at the big square table, with three seated at each of three sides, and no one at the side next to the fireplace. The fireplace was twelve feet wide, and from a distance it was cheerful and sporty, with flame curling around the eight-foot logs their whole length, but my seat at a forward corner of the table was not at a distance. By the time I had finished my clams I was twisting my legs around to the left to keep my pants from blazing up, and my right cheek was about ready for basting. As the soup was being served I twisted the legs still further, and my foot nicked the ankle of my neighbor on the left.

"Sorry," I told him. "What's the name of that animal that can live in fire?"

"Salamander." He was a gravelly tenor, a wiry little specimen with black hair slicked back and broad bulgy shoulders away out of proportion to the rest of him. "What," he asked, "are you doing here?"

"Frying." I turned my head square to him to give my cheek a break. "Please remember this, these may be my last words. My name is Archie Goodwin, and I came here by invitation to bring fourteen things: parsley, onions, chives, chervil, tarragon, fresh mushrooms, brandy, bread crumbs, fresh eggs, paprika, tomatoes, cheese, and Nero Wolfe. That's only thirteen, so I must have left out one. They are ingredients of baked brook trout Montbarry, except the last; Mr. Wolfe is not exactly an ingredient."

He giggled. "I hope not. It would be a very greasy dish, yes?"

"No. That's not fat, it's solid muscle. You should see him lift a pen to sign a letter, absolutely effortless. What are you doing here?"

He tackled his soup and kept at it, so I did likewise. I thought he had crossed me off as a delivery boy, but when his cup was empty he turned to me. "I am an expert, a financier, and a man of guile. I am here—"

"The name first, please. I didn't catch it."

"Certainly, forgive me. Spiros Papps. I am here with my friend, Mr. Theodore Kelefy, the ambassador, to advise him on technical aspects of his mission. I am also here, at this spot, to catch trout, and in the four days we have been here I have caught thirty-eight. Eleven this morning—much better than the ambassador, who got only three. It is claimed that your eastern brook trout, *Salvelinus fontinalis*, is the most savory of all on earth, but I am reserving my opinion until I have tasted one prepared by Mr. Wolfe. Did you say onions?"

"Don't worry," I assured him. "He just waves one at the pan. Do you give advice only to ambassadors, or could I have a little? About these people. The introductions were a little skimpy."

We were interrupted by a servitor with a platter of roast beef, and then one with vegetables, but after that had been attended to he briefed me around the table, keeping his tenor down. O. V. Bragan, the host, was at the best side in the center, the one farthest from the fire. He was a burly six-footer with cold and sharp gray eyes and a square bony chin, somewhere between Wolfe and me in age, and in our brief exchange with him on arrival I had felt no impulse to switch to Hemoco gas, a product of the Hemisphere Oil Company, of which he was it.

Sharing the best side with him, on his right, was Theodore Kelefy, the ambassador. Short but broad, a little pudgy, with no neck to speak of, he looked as if he had been taking on a deep tan for ten years, but it could have been for ten generations. He thought he spoke English, and maybe he did know the words, but he could have used some advice from Spiros Papps on how to pronounce them. On Bragan's other side, his left, was David M. Leeson. If you had looked him over and listened to him—his cool professional smile, his cool cultivated baritone, his cool well-kept and well-handled face—you would have guessed that he was a career diplomat who had worked up to Assistant Secretary of State before he was forty, and you would have hit it right on the nose. It was he who had phoned Wolfe to ask him to cook for his country. One of his footholds on the way up, Spiros Papps told me, had been a couple of years as secretary of the embassy in the capital that Ambassador Kelefy came from.

It helps a career diplomat to have a helpful wife, and, according to Papps, Leeson had one. Papps spoke highly of her, keeping his voice down because she was there on the other side of him, between him and the ambassador. I had no serious objection to her looks, but she had too much forehead for a top rating. Smooth fair skin, light brown hair in a bun, quick brown eyes—that was all very well, but another trouble was the mouth. It had probably started out all right, but something had pulled the corners down. Either she had got bitter about something or she was working too hard on the career. If she had been a little younger I wouldn't have minded finding out which it was and suggesting steps. If Wolfe could serve his country by cooking trout for an ambassador, why couldn't I serve it by perking up the helpful wife of an Assistant Secretary of State?

The other woman at the table didn't need any perking. At the opposite side of the table, kitty-cornered from me, was Adria Kelefy, not the ambassador's daughter, as might have been thought, but his wife. She didn't look especially helpful, but she certainly looked. Small and dark and dainty, with sleepy dark eyes and silky black hair. She was unquestionably fit to pick up and carry somewhere, if only to a drugstore to buy her a Coke, though I doubt if that would have been her idea of a treat. Assistant Secretary Leeson was on her right and Nero Wolfe on her left, and she was going great with both of them. Once she put her hand on Wolfe's arm and kept it there ten seconds, and he didn't pull away. Considering two of his strongest feelings, one about physical contacts and the other about women, I decided it was my duty to get close enough to study her.

But that had to wait. Next to Wolfe, across from me, was the ninth and last, a tall skinny guy with a perpetual squint and a thin tight mouth that was just a hyphen between his bony jaws. His left cheek was four shades redder than his right one, which I understood and sympathized with. The fireplace, on my right, was on his left. His name, Papps said, was James Arthur Ferris. I said he must be something scrubby like a valet or a varlet, since he had been stuck in the other baking seat.

Papps giggled. "Not a valet, not at all. A very important man, Mr. Ferris. I am responsible for his presence. Mr. Bragan would as soon have invited a cobra, but since he had maneuvered to get the ambassador and Secretary Leeson here I thought it only fair that Mr. Ferris should be invited too, and I insisted. Also I am a man of malice. It entertains me to see big men displaying bad blood. You say you are frying. Why are you frying? Because the table is too close to the fire. Why was it placed too close to the fire? So Mr. Bragan could seat Mr. Ferris where he would be highly uncomfortable. No little man is ever as petty as a big man."

My plate empty, I arranged my knife and fork on it according to Hoyle. "Which are you, little or big?"

"Neither. I am unbranded. What you Americans call a maverick."

"What makes Ferris big?"

"He represents big interests—a syndicate of five great oil companies. That is why Mr. Bragan would like to scorch him. Hundreds of millions are at stake. These four days here, we have fished in the morning, squabbled in the afternoon, and fraternized in the evening. Mr. Ferris has gained some ground with the ambassador, but not, I fear, with Secretary Leeson. I find that entertaining. In the end the decision will in effect be mine, and I invite a situation that should mean another ten or twenty million for the government that employs me. If you think I am indiscreet you are wrong. If you repeat what I have said to Mr. Wolfe, and it goes from him to any or all of the others, including Secretary Leeson, I would not reproach you as a chatterbox. I am a man of simple candor. In fact I would go so far as—"

I didn't get to hear how far a man of guile and malice and simple candor would go, on account of an interruption. James Arthur Ferris suddenly shoved his chair back, not quietly, left it, marched the length of the room to the far wall, a good twenty paces, and took a billiard cue from the rack. All heads turned to him, and probably I wasn't alone with my notion that he was going to march back and take a swing at our host, but he merely put the cue ball on the head spot, and, not bothering with any sawing, smashed it into the cluster. The heads turned to Bragan, and then to one another, in dead silence. I grabbed the opportunity. Bragan's scorching Ferris was nothing to me, but scorching me too was uncalled for, and here was my chance. I got up and went to the billiard table and asked Ferris politely, "Shall I rack 'em up and we'll lag for the break?"

He was so damn mad he couldn't speak. He just nodded.

A couple of hours later, going on ten o'clock, Nero Wolfe said to me, "Archie. About your leaving the dinner table. You know what I think of any disturbance at a meal."

"Yes, sir."

We were in his room, bound for bed. Mine was down the hall, and I had stopped in at his by request.

"I concede," he said, "that there may be exceptions, and this was one. Mr. Bragan is either a dunce or a ruffian."

"Yeah. Or both. At least I wasn't tied to a stake—I must remember to thank him. You going fishing tomorrow?"

"You know I'm not." Seated, he grunted as he bent over to unlace his shoes. That done, he straightened. "I inspected the kitchen and equipment, and it will serve. They'll be back at eleven-thirty with the morning's catch, and lunch will be at twelve-thirty. I'll take over the kitchen at ten. The cook is civil and fairly competent. I wish to make an avowal. You were right to oppose this expedition. These people are engaged in bitter and savage combat, with Ambassador Kelefy at the center of it, and in his present humor I doubt if he could distinguish between trout Montbarry and carp fried in lard. As for the others, their mouths would water only at the prospect of long pig. Do you know what that is?"

I nodded. "Cannibal stew. Only each one would want to pick the pig."

"No doubt." He kicked his shoes off. "If we leave immediately after lunch, say three o'clock, will we be home by bedtime?"

I said sure, and told him good night. As I opened the door he spoke to my back, "By the way, it is not lumbago."

## III

The next morning at nine-thirty Wolfe and I had breakfast together at a little table in the big room, by the only window that the sun was hitting through a gap in the trees outside. The griddle cakes were not up to Fritz's by a long shot, but they were edible, and the bacon and maple syrup and coffee were admitted by Wolfe to be a pleasant surprise. The five fishermen had gone off before eight o'clock, each to his assigned stretch of the three miles of private water.

I had my own personal program and had cleared it with our host the evening before. Ever since I caught my first little shiner at the age of seven in an Ohio creek, at sight of wild water I have always had twin feelings: that there must be fish in it, and that they

needed to be taught a lesson. Admitting that the
Crooked River was privately stocked, the fish didn't
know it and were just as cocky as if they had never
been near a hatchery. So I had arranged matters with
Bragan. The five anglers were due back at the lodge
at eleven-thirty, leaving the whole three miles vacant.
Wolfe didn't intend to join them at the lunch table
anyhow, and certainly I wouldn't be missed. I would
have two hours for it, and Bragan told me, though not
very cordially, to help myself to tackle and waders
from the cabinets and drawers.

After breakfast I offered to go and help in the
kitchen, chopping herbs and mushrooms and doing
other chores, but Wolfe said I would only be in the
way, so I went to the cabinets and started poking
around. That was quite a collection, considering that
five men had already helped themselves, presumably
to the best. I finally ended up with a Walton Special
three-piece rod, a Poughqueag reel with a seven-
taper Maxim line, tapered leaders, a fly box with two
dozen assorted flies, a 14-inch willow creel, an alumi-
num-frame net, and Wethersill waders. Assaying at
around four hundred bucks on the hoof, I went to the
kitchen and got three roast-beef sandwiches and a
pair of chocolate bars and stowed them in the creel.

Not bothering to take off the waders, I moseyed
outdoors for a look at the sky and a feel of the wind. It
was a fine day, maybe too fine for good fishing, with a
few white clouds floating high above the pines, not
enough to discourage the sun, and a baby breeze slid-
ing in from the southwest. The river curved around
the lodge in almost a full semicircle, with the lodge's
main veranda, about the size of a tennis court, facing
the big bulge of the curve. I found myself faced with a
problem in etiquette. Toward one end of the veranda,

ten yards to my left, was seated Adria Kelefy, reading a magazine. Toward the other end, ten yards to my right, was seated Sally Leeson, her chin propped on her fist, gazing across the veranda rail at nature. Neither had paid me any visible or audible attention. The problem was, should I wish them good morning, and if so, which one first, the ambassador's wife or the Assistant Secretary of State's wife?

I passed. If they wanted a snubbing contest, okay. But I thought they might as well realize the kind of man they were snubbing, so I acted. There were no trees between the veranda and the river, which wasn't a river at all, merely a creek. From the assortment on the veranda I took an aluminum chair with a canvas seat and high back, carried it down the steps and across the clearing, put it on a level spot ten feet from the creek's edge, got a Gray Hackle from my fly book and put it on the leader, sat in the chair, leaning back to rest my head comfortably, whipped a little line out, dropped the fly onto the ripples, let it float twenty feet downstream, whipped it back gently, and put it out again.

If you ask whether I expected a hit in that unlikely piece of riffle, the answer is yes. I figured that a guy who went to that much trouble to put on an act for the wives of two big men who had snubbed him deserved some co-operation from a mature male trout, and if he deserved it why shouldn't he get it? I might have, too, if Junior hadn't come along and spoiled it. About the twentieth cast my eyes caught a tiny flash and my fingers felt the take, and there I was with Junior on. I gave him the air immediately, hoping he would flop off, but he had it good. If it had been Daddy I could have tired him out, swung him in to me, and taken him off the hook with a dry hand, since he would soon be on the menu, but that little cuss had to be put back with a wet hand. So I had to leave the chair, to dip a hand in the creek before I touched him, which ruined the act.

As I put him back where he belonged, having taught him a lesson, I was considering my position. To return to the chair and carry on as if nothing had happened was out of the question. That damn minnow had made a monkey of me. I might back up in the clearing and do some serious practice casting—but then the sound of steps came, and a voice. "I didn't know you could fish like that from a chair! Where is it?" She said "feesh."

"Good morning, Mrs. Kelefy. I put it back. Too small."

"Oh!" She had reached me. "Let me." She put out a hand. "I'm going to catch one." She looked fully as portable in the strong daylight as she had at night, and the dark eyes just as sleepy. When a woman has eyes like that, a man with any scientific instinct at all wants to find out what it takes to light them up. But a glance at my wrist told me I would be shoving off in eighteen minutes, not time enough to get acquainted and start on research, especially with Sally Leeson sitting there on the veranda gazing, apparently now at us.

I shook my head. "It would be fun to see you catch a fish," I told her, "but I can't give you this rod because it isn't mine. Mr. Bragan lent it to me, and I'm sure he'll lend you one. I'm sorry. To show you how sorry I am, would you care to know one thing I thought as I looked at you last evening at the dinner table?"

"I want to catch a fish. I never saw a fish caught

before." She actually reached to close her fingers on the rod.

I held on. "Mr. Bragan will be here any minute."

"If you give it to me I'll let you tell me what you thought last evening."

I shrugged. "I'm not sure I remember it anyhow. Skip it."

No spark in the eyes. But her hand left the rod and her voice changed a little, person to person. "Of course you remember. What was it?"

"Let's see, how did it go? Oh yes. That big green thing in the ring on your husband's left hand—is it an emerald?"

"Certainly."

"I thought it might be. So I was thinking your husband should display his assets more effectively. With those two assets, the emerald and you, he should have combined them. The best way would be an earring on your right ear, with nothing on the left ear. I had a notion to suggest it to him."

She shook her head. "I wouldn't like it. I like pearls." She reached again for a hold on the rod. "Now I'll catch a fish."

It looked as if we were headed for a tussle, with a good chance of breaking the Walton Special, but an arrival broke it up. James Arthur Ferris, his lanky length fully accoutered, stepped into the clearing and approached, speaking. "Good morning, Mrs. Kelefy! A glorious day, glorious!"

Snubbed again. But I understood; I had beaten him 100 to 46 at the billiard table.

"I want to catch a fish," Mrs. Kelefy told him, "and this man won't give me his rod. I'll take yours."

"Of course," he gushed. "With great pleasure. I

have a Blue Dun on, but if you'd rather try something else—"

I was on my way.

The general run of the creek—all right, river, then —was to the north, but of course it did a lot of twisting and dodging, as shown on a big wall map at the lodge. The three miles of private water were divided into five equal stretches for solo fishing, with the boundaries of the stretches marked by numbered stakes. Two of the stretches were to the south from the lodge, upstream, and the other three to the north, downstream. As arranged the evening before, for that day Spiros Papps and Ambassador Kelefy had the two to the south, and Ferris, Leeson, and Bragan the three to the north.

I am not a dry-fly man, and am no big thrill with a wet fly, so the idea was to start at the upper end and fish downstream, and I headed south on the trail, which, according to the map, more or less ignored the twists of the river and was fairly straight. Less than fifty paces from the lodge I met Spiros Papps, who greeted me with no apparent malice or guile and lifted the lid of his creel to show me seven beauties averaging well over ten inches. A quarter of a mile farther on here came Ambassador Kelefy, who was going to be a little late getting back but nevertheless also had to show me. He had eight, and was pleased to hear that he was one up on Papps.

Starting at the southern boundary of stretch one, I fished back down to the lodge in forty minutes. I prefer to report that forty minutes in bare statistics. Number of flies tried, three. Slips and near-falls, three. Slip and fall, getting wet above the waders, one. Snags of hooks on twigs of overhang, four. Caught, one big enough to keep and five put back.

When I reached the lodge it was just twelve-thirty, lunch time, and I detoured around it to hit stretch three a hundred yards down—the stretch Ferris had fished that morning. There my luck picked up, and in twenty minutes I got three fat ones—one over twelve inches and the other two not much under that. Soon after that I came to a stake with a "4" on it, the start of Assistant Secretary Leeson's stretch. It was a nice spot, with a little patch of grass going right to the edge of the rippling water, and I took off my wet jacket, spread it on a rock in the sun, sat down on another rock, and got out my sandwiches and chocolate.

But I had told Wolfe I would be back by two o'clock, and there was still more than a mile of water to try, so I crammed the grub in, took a couple of swallows of water from the river, which was a creek, put my jacket on, and the creel, and resumed. For the next couple of hundred yards the growth on the banks made it all wading, and the water wasn't the kind trout like to loaf in, but then came a double bend with a long eddy hugging one shore, and I took a stance in the middle, got forty feet of line out, dropped the fly— a Black Gnat—at the top of the eddy, and let it float down. It hadn't gone two feet when Grandpa hit, and I jerked, and I had him on, and here he came upstream, straight for me, which is of course one of the disadvantages of working downstream. I managed to keep line on him, and when he was damn near close enough to bite me he suddenly made a U turn and off he went, back into the eddy, right on through it, and around the second bend. Not having a mile of line, I went splashing after him without stopping to test footholds, up to my knees and then to my thighs and then to my knees again, until I could see around the bend. It was a straight piece of rough water, thirty feet wide, dotted with boulders, and I was heading for one to use as a brace in the current when I saw something that halted me. A boulder near the bank was already being used as a brace if my eyes were any good, and they were. Keeping a bent rod on Grandpa, I worked over to the boulder near the bank. It was Assistant Secretary Leeson. His feet and shanks were on the bank; his knees were at the edge of the water; and the rest of him was in the water, lodged against the upstream side of the boulder. The force of the current was gently bobbing him up and down, so that one moment his face was visible and the next moment it wasn't.

Even one brief glimpse of the face was enough to answer the main question, but there is always the chance in a million, so I straightened up to reel my line in, and at that instant the fish broke water for the first time. He came clear out and on up to do a flip, and I couldn't believe it. There was a smaller one than him on a plank displayed in the lodge. Instinctively, of course, I gave him line when I saw him take the air, and when he was back under I took it in and had him bending the rod again.

"Damn it," I said aloud, "it's a dilemma."

I transferred the rod to my left hand with the line pinched between the tips of the thumb and index finger of that hand, made sure of good footing, stooped and gripped the collar of Leeson's jacket with my right hand, lifted his head clear of the water, and took a look. That was enough. Even if he wasn't drowned he wasn't alive. I backed up slowly out onto the bank, taking him along, and as I let him down and his shoulders touched the ground the trout broke water again.

Ordinarily such a fish would rate fifteen or twenty

minutes of careful handling, but under the circumstances I was naturally a little impatient, and it
wasn't more than half of that before I worked him in
to where I could get him in the net. He was seven
inches longer than the width of the creel, and I hated
to bend him but had to. I took another look at
Leeson's head, and, when I moved him a little further
from the water, I put my handkerchief under it so it
wouldn't be in contact with the ground. I covered the
upper third of him with my jacket, took my rod apart,
and looked at my watch. Twenty past one. That was
all right; the trout Montbarry would be gone by the
time I got there. Wolfe would be sore enough as it
was, but I would never have heard the last of it if I
had arrived in the middle of that particular meal to
announce a corpse. I hit the trail, with the rod in one
hand and the creel in the other.

It was a lot quicker to the lodge by the trail than it
had been wading down. As I emerged from the trees
into the clearing I saw that lunch was over, for they
were all out on the veranda having coffee—the four
men and two women. Mounting the steps and heading
for the door, I thought I was going to be snubbed
again, but O. V. Bragan called to me. "Goodwin! Did
you see Secretary Leeson anywhere?"

"No." I kept going.

"Didn't you fish his stretch?"

"Only part of it." I halted long enough to add, "I
got wet and need a change," and then went on. Inside
I made for the kitchen. The cook and two waiters
were seated at a table, eating. I asked where Wolfe
was, and they said in his room, so I backtracked, took
the hall to the other wing, found Wolfe's door standing
open, and entered. He was putting something in his
suitcase, which was open on the bed.

"You're early," he grunted. "Satisfactory."

"Yes, sir. I've got four trout and one supertrout to take back to Fritz, as promised. How was the lunch?"

"Passable. I cooked twenty trout and they were all eaten. I'm nearly packed, and we can go. Now."

"Yes, sir. First I have a report. About three-quarters of a mile downstream I found Secretary Leeson against a boulder near the bank, his feet out of the water and the rest of him in. He had been there some time; his armpits were good and cold."

"Good heavens." Wolfe was scowling at me. "You would. Drowned?"

"I don't know. I—"

"You have told Mr. Bragan."

"No, sir. I'm reporting to you. I removed it from the water to the bank. His skull was smashed in, back of the right ear and above it, by a blow or blows, I would say with a rock or a heavy club. Not from a fall, not a chance, unless he climbed to the top of a high tree to fall from, and there's none there high enough. Somebody clobbered him. So I thought you should be present when I announce it, preferably with your eyes open."

"Pfui. You think he was murdered."

"Twenty to one, at least."

His lips tightened and the scowl deepened. "Very well. They'll find him soon. They thought he was being stubborn about filling his creel and decided to go and look for him after lunch. Since he was mostly under water you didn't have to see him—no, confound it, you took him out. Even so, get those things off and dress. We are leaving. I don't intend—"

"No, sir." I was firm. "As you say, I took him out. They know I fished that stretch. We probably wouldn't even get home. We'd get stopped somewhere around Albany and brought back, and then where would we spend the night? One guess."

He took in air, a sigh that filled him clear down to his waistline. When it was out again he blurted savagely, "Why the devil did you have to go fishing?" He sighed again. "Go and tell Mr. Bragan."

"Yes, sir. You're coming along?"

"No! Why should I? I am not concerned. Go!"

I was sweating under the waders, so I peeled them off and slipped my shoes on before I went. When I got to the veranda three of the men—Bragan, Ferris, and Papps—had left it and were crossing the clearing to the trail, and I sung out, "Bragan! You three come back here please?"

He called, astonished, "What for? We're going to find Leeson!"

"I already found him. Come here and I'll tell you."

"Found him where?"

"I said come here."

Wolfe may not have cared about seeing their faces as I gave them the news, but I did. All of them. I ignored Bragan's demands until the three of them had mounted the steps and were facing me in a group that included Ambassador Kelefy and the two women.

"I did see Secretary Leeson," I told them. "I went to tell Mr. Wolfe first because I thought he might want to tell you, but he leaves it to me. Leeson is dead." I stopped.

Spiros Papps, standing next to Sally Leeson, took hold of her arm. She just stared at me. Adria Kelefy's mouth fell open. Ferris and Ambassador Kelefy made noises, and Bragan demanded, "Dead? How? Where?"

"I found his body on the river bank with most of him in the water, including his head. I lifted him out, but he had been dead some time." I focused on Bragan. "You'll get a doctor of course, but also you'll have to get the police, and the body must not be moved again until they come, because—"

Sally Leeson pulled away from Papps and made a dash for the steps. I jumped and grabbed her and got my arms around her. "Hold on a minute," I told her, "and I'll take you there if you have to go. Just hold on."

"Why the police?" Bragan demanded.

"His skull is smashed. Don't argue with me, save it for them. I'm going back to the body and stay there till they come. Shall I call them first?"

"No. I will."

"And a doctor."

"Yes."

"Good. It's at the double bend two hundred yards below the number four stake." I loosened my grip on the widow, and she was stiff and straight. "You'd better stay here, Mrs. Leeson."

"No. I must . . . take me."

"Then I'd just as soon have someone along. Ferris?"

"No."

"Kelefy?"

"I think not."

"Papps?"

"Certainly," he said politely, and the three of us went.

IV

Two hours later, at a quarter to four, it was a convention.

Two state troopers had been the first to arrive, and Bragan had brought them down to us at the double bend. Soon after, the doctor came, and, while he was no metropolitan medical examiner, he did have his head along. When he asked me why I had put my handkerchief under Leeson's head, and I said because I thought the water might not have washed away all evidence of what it was that had smashed the skull, he said that was very sensible and it was too bad he didn't have a good glass with him. But his main contribution was to make it official that Leeson was dead, and to insist that Mrs. Leeson let Papps take her back to the lodge. The body couldn't be moved until the sheriff came.

When the sheriff arrived he had two county detectives along. Then more troopers, including a lieutenant. Then the district attorney, a bouncy bald guy named Jasper Colvin, with rimless spectacles that he had to shove back on his nose every time he took a step. He had two underlings with him. Then a couple of journalists, one with a notebook and one with a camera. They all got around to me, and they all seemed to have the idea that I was leaving something out, but that was nothing new. Any officer of the law would rather be caught dead than admit he believes that you're telling him the truth, the whole truth, and nothing but.

When a stretcher finally came for the remains most of the public servants were scattered around looking for the weapon or other relevant items, and my offer to help carry was accepted. It was quite a load and quite a portage. After we had lifted the stretcher into an ambulance that had squeezed onto the edge of the crowded parking space back of the lodge, I circled around to the veranda and found no one there but a trooper standing biting his lip. Inside, in the big room, Ferris and Papps were on chairs by a window having a conversation, and a stranger was at a table using the phone.

Papps called to me. "Anything new?"

"Not with me," I told him, and crossed to the inner hall.

Wolfe was in his room, in the chair with rainbow rugs, with a book. He shot me a glance as I entered and then went back to the book. I stood. "Do you want a report?"

His eyes stayed on the page. "Not unless it bears upon our leaving here."

"It doesn't. Any questions or instructions?"

"No."

"You know damn well," I said pleasantly, "that you approved of my going fishing. Where are my trout?"

"In the kitchen in the large refrigerator. Cleaned."

"Thank you very much." I left him and went to my room.

I was there an hour later when a trooper came to tell me I was wanted. I supposed it was for more of the same, but Wolfe was in the hall outside his door, and started off as I approached, and led the way to the big room, with the trooper in the rear.

It looked as if something was stewing. The five guests were in a group, seated, in the middle of the room, and Bragan was standing nearby talking with District Attorney Colvin. The sheriff and two troopers were over near the door, and one of the pair the DA had brought with him was seated at a little table with an open notebook before him. Three paces in Wolfe stopped and raised his voice. "You sent for me, Mr. Bragan?"

Colvin answered. "I did. I'm Jasper Colvin, district attorney of this county." He pushed his specs back up on his nose. "You're Nero Wolfe, a private detective?"

"Yes."

"You will sit here, please. You too, Goodwin. I have something to say to all of you."

I wouldn't have been surprised if Wolfe had about-faced and marched out, since he had had three provocations: first, Colvin's tone of voice; second, his saying "*a* private detective," not "*the* private detective"; and third, the size of the chair indicated, at the rear of the group of guests. But after a second's hesitation he went and sat, and I took the other vacant chair next to him.

The DA stood facing his audience. He cleared his throat. "I am sure, ladies and gentlemen, I don't need—"

"Want me to take this?" It was the man at the table with the notebook.

Colvin turned his head to snap, "Yes, everything!" and turned back. He pushed the specs back and cleared his throat again. "I don't need to tell you, ladies and gentlemen, how painful I find my duty today. But just as Assistant Secretary of State Leeson, at his high level, always put his duty as diplomat and statesman first, so must I, in my much humbler capacity, do likewise. I know you all appreciate that."

They didn't say. He went on. "When I arrived here on this tragic mission, two hours ago, I found that Sheriff Dell and Lieutenant Hopp were already here, and I consulted with them. We agreed that there was no point in harassing you until certain lines of investigation had been tried, and you were merely asked a few routine questions and requested to remain on the premises for possible further inquiry. In that connection I wish to convey the sincere thanks of myself personally, and of the people of the state of New York, to Ambassador Kelefy. He and his wife, and Mr. Spiros Papps of his staff, are protected by diplomatic immunity from arrest or detention, but they have made no objection to our request. I may say that I have phoned the State Department in Washington for advice in this matter."

"That wasn't necessary," Kelefy assured him. "Even diplomats are human occasionally." His pronunciation was no better under stress, but I won't try to spell it.

Colvin nodded at him, and down came the specs. After pushing them up the DA resumed. "But now it is my painful duty to tell you that we will have to go further than routine questions, on account of certain aspects the matter has taken on. We have had to reject the idea that Secretary Leeson's death was accidental. Two doctors agree that the injury to the skull could not have been caused by any conceivable accident at that spot. They also agree that it couldn't possibly have been self-inflicted. Therefore it was homicide."

Since Wolfe and I were in the rear I couldn't see their faces, and the backs of their heads weren't very expressive. The only one that moved was James Arthur Ferris. He turned his head for a glance at Sally Leeson.

O. V. Bragan spoke up. "I'd like to comment on that."

"Go ahead, Mr. Bragan."

"I told you when you got here it might be murder. I reminded you and the troopers that I've been bothered with poachers on my water, and I suggested that you immediately start your men investigating the possibility that Leeson came on one at the river and was attacked by him. Did you do that?"

Colvin cleared his throat and had to push the specs. "We didn't overlook that possibility, Mr. Bragan, but permit me to finish. An examination of the skull wound with a magnifying glass disclosed three particles of wood bark that had not been dislodged by the water. That justified the assumption that the blow or blows had been struck with a wooden club. If so, where was it? It wasn't at or near the spot. It seemed unlikely that the assailant had carried it away. Probably he had thrown it from him, and most probably, he had thrown it in the river. And it has been found—or I should say, a club has been found. Bring it here, Nate."

The sheriff walked over to him and held it up. It was three feet long, maybe a little more, as thick as my arm.

"It was found," Colvin said, "in the river five hundred feet downstream from the bend, wedged between two rocks where the current had carried it. It's ash. The water was playing over it, but the bark wasn't soaked through, so it hadn't been there very long. As you see, it was sawed off at both ends. Near one end the bark is bruised for three or four inches as if it had hit something hard. It will take a microscope to find out if the water left any evidence in the bruised bark, but we think we are justified in assuming that that club was the weapon. And you must permit me, Mr. Bragan, you must permit me to say that if Secretary Leeson surprised a poacher on your water, I can conceive of no reason why the poacher was carrying such a club. Sheriff Dell and Lieutenant Hopp agree with me."

"You don't have to conceive his reason," Bragan rumbled. "Find him and ask him."

"That is a possibility," the DA conceded. "Two of the sheriff's men and two troopers are now exploring it. But one more fact. There are two large stacks of firewood outside on your premises. One of them is eight-foot logs for your big fireplace. The other is shorter and smaller logs for the smaller fireplaces in your other rooms, and in it are scores, hundreds, of pieces of ash similar to the one the sheriff has just shown you. There is no stack of wood like that within two miles or more. So believe me, Mr. Bragan, we have been forced to our conclusion, we don't like it, we don't like it at all, but duty is duty no matter how painful it is. Our conclusion is that Secretary Leeson was killed with that club by premeditation, that the club came from your woodpile, and that it was used by someone here at your place. Is that right, Nate?"

"That's the way I see it," the sheriff declared.

"Right, Lieutenant?"

"It seems," the trooper allowed, "to fit the facts as a basis for inquiry."

Bragan was leaning forward. "You're actually saying that I or one of my guests murdered Secretary Leeson? And you know who my guests are?"

"I certainly do." Colvin pushed the specs. I'll only mention it every fourth or fifth time. "But there are two of them who may have reason to—" He stopped. "No." He turned to the man with the notebook. "Strike that last sentence."

"Okay." The man scratched with his pen.

Colvin resumed. "I am keenly aware of the situation, Mr. Bragan, but the inquiry must be proper and of course unprejudiced. It may be necessary later to talk with one or more of you privately, but I think it's better to start this way, with you first, naturally. For the record, I ask you, did you strike Leeson with that club or any other weapon?"

"No. Good God. No."

"Have you any reason whatever to suspect any person present of having done so?"

"No. None."

Colvin's eyes moved. Specs back. "Those two questions are pro forma for each and all of you. You have heard them and will please answer them. Mrs. Leeson?"

"No." Her voice was low but firm. "To both."

"Mrs. Kelefy?"

"One moment," Ferris put in. "To put such questions to the wife of a distinguished foreign ambassador is highly improper."

I would have liked to ask if it would be okay to put them to the wife of an undistinguished foreign ambassador, but skipped it. Anyway, the distinguished ambassador was speaking. "This is no time to seek refuge in propriety. Answer, my dear."

"But of course," she said. I would have liked to see her eyes. "Certainly no to both questions."

"Ambassador Kelefy, if you wish to answer?"

"I do. I answer no."

"Mr. Papps?"

"No and no."

"Mr. Ferris?"

"No to both."

"Nero Wolfe?"

"No."

"To both?"

"Yes."

"Goodwin?"

"I've been asked before. No again, twice."

Colvin's eyes went right and left. "You were asked previously when and where you last saw Secretary Leeson alive, but under the present circumstances I would like to verify it. Ambassador Kelefy and Mr. Papps, whose stretches were south, upstream, last saw him when they parted from him on the veranda shortly before eight o'clock this morning. Mrs. Leeson last saw him when he left their room this morning to go to breakfast. Mrs. Kelefy last saw him last evening when she and her husband left this room to go to bed. Mr. Ferris last saw him on the trail, when Mr. Ferris left the trail to strike the river and start fishing his stretch, number three, upstream. Secretary Leeson and Mr. Bragan continued on the trail, and Mr. Bragan last saw him when he left the trail for the river at the beginning of his stretch, number four. Mr. Bragan continued on the trail to the boundary of his water, to fish stretch number five. Wolfe and Goodwin last saw him last evening in this room. That's the way we have it, that's what you've told us. I now ask each and all of you, is that correct in every particular? Correct not only as regards yourself, but as regards the others? If not, tell me."

Not a peep. Colvin took a breath. Specs. "Mr. Bragan, it is necessary to ask you this. There was a piece in the paper day before yesterday, a dispatch from Washington, about this fishing party at your lodge. Naturally I read it with interest, since this is my county. It said that Ambassador Kelefy's chief purpose in his new post would be to carry on negotiations regarding oil rights in his country, that vast sums were involved, and that he had brought Mr. Spiros Papps with him for that purpose; that Assistant Secretary Leeson was included in the party because he knew Ambassador Kelefy, having formerly been secretary of our embassy in the ambassador's country; and that the negotiations might be brought to a conclusion on the bank of this trout stream, since the two chief bidders for the rights were both here. The article named them: O. V. Bragan of the Hemisphere Oil Company and James Arthur Ferris of the Universal Syndicate."

"Well, what about it?"

"It was an Associated Press dispatch, so it went all over the country. It said the rivalry between Hemisphere and Universal was intense and bitter—yes, it said bitter. I don't imply anything, anything at all, but you must see that this is going to cause immediate and widespread speculation. Do you want to comment on that?"

"I do not."

"It might be helpful for you to give me some idea, privately if you prefer, of the state of the negotiations. Of the nature of the relationships of all those concerned. It might help to eliminate that as—uh—as a factor."

"It's already eliminated. You're beyond your depth, Colvin."

"You certainly are." Ferris was supporting his bitter rival. "This is preposterous. Go find the poacher."

"If I may," Ambassador Kelefy put in diplomatically. "I agree with Mr. Bragan and Mr. Ferris. Americans do not fight even for millions with clubs."

I could have named him an American who had used a blackjack on a fellow citizen to relieve him of $2.38, but of course he wasn't an oil tycoon.

"You're not only beyond your depth," Bragan told the DA, "but you're too free with conclusions. Even if that club was the weapon and it came from my woodpile, and therefore it was premeditated, why was it one of us? Anyone could sneak in through the woods and get a stick from the woodpile."

"True," Colvin agreed. "Quite true. But it must have been premeditated, and Secretary Leeson must have been a chosen target. As I said, four trained men are exploring that possibility. But the laws of probability compel us to center our attention on this place and the people here. By no means exclusively on you and your five guests; there are five others. Wolfe, Goodwin, and your three servants. The three servants have been questioned, and we're certainly not through with them. I want to ask you about them. The cook's name is Michael Samek?"

"Yes. This is ridiculous. Mike has been with me for fifteen years—at my home in New York, in Florida in the winter. The other—"

"Isn't that a Russian name? Is he a Russian?"

"No. He's an American. You certainly are seeing things, Colvin. He was born in Buffalo. The other two men are from an agency in New York and I have used them many times. For years. Do you want the name of the agency?"

"We got it from them. Have you any reason whatever to suppose that one of those three might be involved in this?"

"I have not. I have every reason to suppose they aren't."

"All right, but you understand they have to be thoroughly checked. Now about Wolfe and Goodwin. The newspaper article said that Wolfe was coming to cook trout for Ambassador Kelefy. Is that correct?"

"Yes."

"Did you arrange that?"

"No. Secretary Leeson did."

"When did they get here?"

"Late yesterday afternoon, just before dinner."

"Why did Goodwin come along?"

"I suppose to drive the car. Ask him."

"I intend to. But first please tell me—to your knowledge, was there anything behind that arrangement? Some other reason for getting Wolfe and Goodwin here?"

"No. Not to my knowledge."

"Then if there was some secret reason, some ulterior motive, for the arrangement, it was known only to Secretary Leeson, who is now dead?"

"I can't say. It wasn't known to me."

Colvin's eyes went to Wolfe, and he raised his chin and his voice. "I ask you, Wolfe. Goodwin says that the arrangement for your coming here was made on the telephone with Secretary Leeson. Have you any record other than your own memory of what was said on the telephone?"

If he had worked at it for a week he couldn't have thought up a worse approach.


V


Wolfe, beside me, sat slowly moving his head from side to side, and I thought he was simply going to clam up and let it go at that. But no. He spoke. "It's too bad, Mr. Colvin."

"What's too bad?"

"That you're spoiling it. You people have investigated promptly and efficiently, and you have expounded the situation admirably—though I think 'assumptions' would be a better word than 'conclusions' at this stage. You even show—"

"I asked you a question! Answer it!"

"I shall. You even show commendable spunk in dealing with two billionaires and an ambassador, and I can't blame you for wanting to impress them by using a sharper tone and a more pugnacious manner for me. Though I don't blame you, I would certainly tell you to go to the devil but for the fact that my one desire is to leave here and go home. So I suggest a *modus operandi*. I will make a statement—you have a stenographer there. When I'm through you may ask questions, and I may answer them."

"I've asked one. You can answer that."

Wolfe shook his head patiently. "I've offered a statement. Isn't that accepted procedure?"

The sheriff, who had returned to the group by the door, called over, "Maybe he'd like it better at the courthouse!"

The DA ignored it. He pushed his specs back up. "Go ahead and make your statement."

"Yes, sir." Wolfe was trying not to be smug. He did want to go home. "Eleven days ago I had a telephone call from Washington and was told that Mr. David M. Leeson, Assistant Secretary of State, wished to speak with me. Mr. Leeson, whom I had never met, told me that a fishing party was being arranged for Ambassador Kelefy, newly arrived in this country, and that the ambassador had expressed a desire to eat fresh trout cooked by Nero Wolfe, and would I oblige him. Mr. Leeson said it would be deeply appreciated. I was engaged on a difficult job and reserved my decision. Mr. Leeson phoned me again two days later, and again three days later, and I agreed to go, and he gave me the necessary information. No other matter was mentioned by either of us in any of the conversations."

"Did Leeson write you about it?"

"No. It was all arranged on the phone. Yesterday morning Mr. Goodwin and I left my house in New York and drove here in my car, arriving around six o'clock. He accompanied me because he always does, and I had so stipulated with Mr. Leeson. He and I dined in this room with the others, and went to our rooms and to bed about ten o'clock. Neither of us had ever before met any of the people here, and neither of us had any private conversation with any of them yesterday or during the night. This morning we arose rather late and breakfasted together in this room at half past nine; we were told that the others, the five men, had all gone fishing before eight o'clock. After breakfast I went to the kitchen to start preparations for cooking lunch, and Mr. Goodwin got himself outfitted for fishing. From that point the account of Mr. Goodwin's movements will come from him; no doubt he has already furnished it. I stayed in the kitchen until luncheon had been cooked and served; I ate mine in the kitchen; and a little after one o'clock I went to my room and remained there until Mr. Goodwin arrived and told me he had found Mr. Leeson's body."

"What time was it—"

"If you please. A little more. You hinted at the possibility—delicately, but you did hint it—of a connection between the attack on Mr. Leeson and the contest for the oil rights which Ambassador Kelefy is negotiating. As the investigation gets hotter I suppose you'll return to that, in private interviews, and sooner or later someone will certainly mention an incident that occurred in this room last evening at the dinner table. Mr. Goodwin might, since he was casually involved. So I mention it now. Mr. Bragan placed the table, and arranged the seating, so that Mr. Ferris and Mr. Goodwin were toasted before our eyes. Their only alternatives were discourtesy or cremation, and they chose the former; they left the table and played billiards. I don't suggest that this has any bearing on the murder; I report it only because it was a notable incident and I don't want to be reproached later for leaving it out."

Wolfe closed his eyes and opened them again. "That's all, I think, except to add that I fully realize the pickle you're in. You are driven to the hypothesis that someone on these premises is a murderer. Eleven of us. The three servants are probably hopeless. Leaving eight. Mrs. Leeson seems highly unlikely. Leaving seven. Ambassador Kelefy, his wife, and Mr. Papps are beyond your reach even for inquisition, let alone indictment. Leaving four. Mr. Bragan and Mr. Ferris are mighty men of great wealth, dangerous to offend without the most conclusive grounds; you will provoke them at your peril. Leaving two, Mr. Goodwin and me. So I understand your eagerness to impeach us, but it's no good. Don't waste time and energy on us."

"Are you through?"

"Yes. If you wish a statement from Mr. Goodwin also, he—"

"We already have Goodwin's story. Naturally it agrees with yours." The DA's tone indicated no desire for peaceful coexistence. "For the record, I deny your allegation that we are eager to impeach you, as you put it. We are eager for only one thing, the truth about the commission of this crime. You say you went to the kitchen, parting from Goodwin, immediately after breakfast?"

"Yes."

"And that was around ten o'clock?"

"Almost precisely at ten."

"When did you see him next?"

"Shortly before eleven o'clock he came to the kitchen and got sandwiches for his lunch, and left. The next time was when he came to my room and told me of finding Mr. Leeson's body."

Colvin nodded. "Around one-thirty." Specs. "Goodwin admits he was alone for forty minutes or more after you went to the kitchen. He says he was in this room, looking over the tackle and getting himself equipped, but he had ample time to slip out the side door, make his way to stretch four, find Secretary Leeson and deal with him, return, and proceed to the veranda to register his presence with Mrs. Kelefy and Mrs. Leeson. Or, as an alternative, he had reason to suppose that Secretary Leeson would stay out beyond the appointed hour, and, after starting south and meeting Mr. Papps and Ambassador Kelefy on the trail, he doubled back through the woods, detouring around the lodge, found Secretary Leeson, even possibly by previous arrangement, and killed him."

Wolfe's brows were up. "Had he gone mad? I grant that Mr. Goodwin sometimes acts impulsively, but that seems rather extreme."

"Murder is extreme." Colvin's voice went up a notch. "You can save your sarcasm, Wolfe. I understand it goes over big in New York, but here upstate we don't appreciate it. If Goodwin did it he had a motive, sure, and I can't produce it now, but there are plenty of possibilities. You like money. What if Secretary Leeson was in somebody's way, and that somebody came and offered you a big sum to help dispose of him? He knew you had been asked to come here, and that would give you and Goodwin a perfect opportunity. So you decided to come, and you did. It doesn't have to be that Goodwin suddenly went mad, or you either."

"Pfui." Wolfe sighed. "Wild conjectures have their place in an investigation, Mr. Colvin, no doubt of that, but it is better not to blab them until they are supported by some slender thread of fact. That's mere moonshine. You have my statement. You may indulge yourself in fantastic nonsense, but don't pester me with it. Let's be explicit. Are you calling me a liar?"

"I am!"

"Then there's no point in going on." Wolfe left his chair, which had been supporting about 80 per cent of his fanny. "I'll be in my room, with no interest in any further communication except word that I may leave for home. Since you already have Mr. Goodwin's story, you won't need him either. Come, Archie." He moved.

"Wait a minute!" Colvin commanded. "I'm not through with you! Is your statement absolutely complete?"

Wolfe, having taken a step, halted and turned his head. "Yes."

"You included a notable incident. That's what you called it. Was there any other notable incident that you didn't mention?"

"No. None that I know about."

"None whatever?"

"No."

"Then you don't call it notable that you came here to cook trout for Ambassador Kelefy, that's what you came for, and when they brought in their creels today and you and the cook cleaned the trout, you did *not* include the trout in Ambassador Kelefy's creel? The trout he had caught himself? You don't call that notable?"

Wolfe's shoulders went up a quarter of an inch and down again. "Not especially."

"Well, I do." Colvin was bearing down, quite nasty. "The cook, Samek, says that the creels were tagged with the names. You selected the fish from them. Bragan's had ten and you used nine of them. Ferris's had nine and you used six. Papps's had seven and you used five. Ambassador Kelefy's had eight, all of good size, and you didn't use one of them. They were still there in the kitchen and Samek showed them to me. Nothing wrong with them as far as I could see. Do you deny this?"

"Oh no." I caught a little gleam in Wolfe's eye. "But will you tell me how it relates to the crime you're investigating?"

"I don't know. But I call it a notable incident and you didn't mention it." Colvin's head moved. "Ambassador Kelefy, if you will permit me, did you know that Wolfe didn't cook any of the fish you caught?"

"No, Mr. Colvin, I didn't. This is rather a surprise."

"Do you know of any reason for it? Does any occur to you?"

"I'm afraid not." Kelefy swiveled his head for a glance at Wolfe, and back to the DA. "No doubt Mr. Wolfe can supply one."

"He certainly can. What about it, Wolfe? Why?"

Wolfe shook his head. "Relate it to the murder, Mr. Colvin. I shouldn't withhold evidence, of course, but I'm not; the trout are there; scrutinize them, dissect them, send them to the nearest laboratory for full analysis. I resent your tone, your diction, your manners, and your methods; and only a witling would call a man with my conceit a liar. Come, Archie."

I can't say how it would have developed if there

hadn't been a diversion. As Wolfe made for the door
to the hall with me at his heels, the sheriff, the lieutenant, and the other trooper came trotting across to
head us off, and they succeeded, since Wolfe had neither the build nor the temperament to make a dash
for it. But only two of them blocked the doorway because as they came the phone rang and the lieutenant
changed course to go to the table and answer it. After
a word he turned to call to the DA. "For you, Mr.
Colvin. Attorney General Jessel."

Colvin went to get it, leaving the two groups—the
six on chairs in the middle of the room, and us four
standing at the door—stuck in tableaux. The conversation wasn't long, and he had the short end of it.
When he hung up he turned, pushed back the specs,
and announced, "That was Mr. Herman Jessel, attorney general of the state of New York. I phoned him
just before calling you together here and described
the situation. He has talked with Governor Holland,
and is leaving Albany immediately to come here, and
wants me to postpone further questioning of you ladies and gentlemen until he arrives. That will probably be around eight o'clock. Meanwhile we will pursue
certain other lines of inquiry. Lieutenant Hopp has
established a cordon outside to exclude intruders, especially representatives of the press. You are requested to remain inside the lodge or on the veranda."

He pushed the specs back up.

# VI

Wolfe sat in the rainbow chair in his room, leaning
back, his eyes closed, his lips compressed, his fingers

folded at the apex of his middle mound. I stood at a
window, looking out. Fifty paces away, at the edge of
the woods, a trooper was standing, gazing up at a
tree. I focused on it, thinking a journalist might be
perched on an upper branch, but it must have been a
squirrel or a bird.

Wolfe's voice sounded behind me. "What time is
it?"

"Twenty after five." I turned.

"Where would we be if we had left at two o'clock?"

"On Route Twenty-two four miles south of
Hoosick Falls."

"Bosh. You can't know that."

"That's what I do know. What I don't know is why
you didn't let the ambassador eat his trout."

"Thirty-four were caught. I cooked twenty. That's
all."

"Okay, save it. What I don't know won't hurt me.
I'll tell you what I think. I think the guy that sent us
here to kill Leeson was sending you messages by putting them inside trout and tossing the trout in the
river, and some of them were in the ones Kelefy
caught, and you had to wait for a chance to get them
out when the cook wasn't looking, and when—"

There was a knock at the door and I went and
opened it, and O. V. Bragan, our host, stepped in. No
manners. When I shut the door and turned he was
already across to Wolfe and talking. "I want to ask
you about something."

Wolfe opened his eyes. "Yes, Mr. Bragan? Don't
stand on ceremony. Indeed, don't stand at all. Looking
up at people disconcerts me. Archie?"

I moved a chair up for the burly six-footer, expecting no thanks and getting none. There are two kinds
of executives, thankers and non-thankers, and I al-

ready had Bragan tagged. But since Wolfe had taken a crack at him about ceremony I thought I might as well too, and told him not to mention it. He didn't hear me.

His cold and sharp gray eyes were leveled at Wolfe. "I liked the way you handled Colvin," he stated.

Wolfe grunted. "I didn't. I want to go home. When I talk with a man who is in a position to give me something I want, and I don't get it, I have blundered. I should have toadied him. Vanity comes high."

"He's a fool."

"I don't agree." Obviously Wolfe was in no mood to agree with anyone or anything. "I thought he did moderately well. For an obscure official in a remote community his stand with Mr. Ferris and you was almost intrepid."

"Bah. He's a fool. The idea that anyone here would deliberately murder Leeson is so damned absurd that only a fool would take it seriously."

"Not as absurd as the idea that a poacher, with a club from your woodpile as a cane, was struck with the fancy of using it as a deadly weapon. Discovered poachers don't kill; they run."

"All right, it wasn't a poacher." Bragan was brusque. "And it wasn't anyone here. But God knows what this is going to mean to my plans. If it isn't cleared up in a hurry anything can happen. With Leeson murdered here at my lodge, the State Department could decide to freeze me out, and not only that, Ambassador Kelefy could decide he'd rather not deal with me, and that would be worse."

He hit his chair arm with a fist. "It has *got* to be cleaned up in a hurry! And God knows it won't be, the way they're going at it. I know your reputation some,

Wolfe, and I just spoke on the phone with one of my associates in New York. He says you're straight, and you're good, and you charge exorbitant fees. To hell with that. If this thing drags along and ruins my plans I'll lose a thousand times more than any fee you ever charged. I want you to go to work on this. I want you to find out who killed Leeson, and damned quick."

"Sitting here?" Wolfe was bored. "Confined to the lodge and veranda? Another absurd idea."

"You wouldn't be. Jessel, the attorney general, will be here in a couple of hours. I know him well, I made a little contribution to his campaign. After I talk with him and he reads your statement, and questions you if he wants to, he'll let you go. I've got a plane at a landing field twelve miles from here, and you and Goodwin will fly to Washington and get busy. I'll give you some names of people there that can help, and I'll phone them from here. The way it looks to me, somebody that wanted to finish Leeson decided to do it here. You find him and pin it on him, and quick. I'm not telling you how; that's your job. Well?"

"No," Wolfe said bluntly.

"Why not?"

"It doesn't appeal to me."

"To hell with appeal. Why not?"

"I am responsible for my decisions, Mr. Bragan, but to myself, not to you. However, I am your guest. I would ride in an airplane only in desperation, and I am not desperate. Again, I want to go home, and Washington is not my home. Again, even if your assumption regarding the murder were correct, it might take so long to find him and expose him that your plans would be beyond salvage. There is a fourth reason even more cogent than those, but I'm not prepared to disclose it."

"What is it?"

"No, sir. You're an overbearing man, Mr. Bragan, but I'm a dogged man. I owe you the decent courtesy of a guest, but that's all, and I decline the job. Archie, someone at the door."

I was on my way to answer the knock. This time, getting adapted to the etiquette of the place and not wanting to be trampled, I backed up with the door as I opened it, and sure enough, he breezed right in and on past me. It was James Arthur Ferris. Bragan was sitting with his back to the door. When Ferris got far enough to see who it was, he stopped and blurted, "You here, Bragan? Good."

Bragan blurted back, "Why is it good?"

"Because I was coming to ask Wolfe and Goodwin for a little favor. I was going to ask them to come with me to your room and be present while I said something to you. I've learned from experience that it's advisable to have witnesses present when I'm talking with you."

"Oh, for God's sake come off it." Bragan was fed up. First Wolfe turning him down flat, and now this. "There's been a murder. A statesman has been murdered. On every radio and TV network, and tomorrow on the front page of a thousand papers. Pull in your horns!"

Ferris, not listening apparently, was squinting down at Wolfe. "If you don't mind," he said, "I'll say it here. There's no danger that you'll ever have to testify to it or even furnish an affidavit, because Bragan hasn't got the guts to lie when he knows it's three to one. I'll appreciate the favor." He turned the squint on Bragan, and you wouldn't think his thin little hyphen of a mouth was much to show hate with, but he certainly managed it. "I just want to tell you what I'm going to do, so you can't say afterwards that it hit you without warning."

"Go ahead." Bragan's head was tilted back to face the squint. "Let's hear it."

"As you know, the attorney general is on his way here. He's going to ask about the status of our negotiations with Kelefy and Papps, and where Leeson stood. He may not think that had any connection with the murder, but he's certainly going to ask about it, and not in a meeting like that Colvin, but each of us privately. When he asks me I'm going to tell him."

"What are you going to tell him?"

"I'm going to tell him the truth. How you had your Paris man working on Kelefy and Papps before they even left home. How you tried to get something on Papps. How you had that woman on the plane with them to try to work on Mrs. Kelefy, only it didn't go. How you had two men I can name trying to put screws on Leeson, and—"

"Watch it, Ferris. I advise you to watch it. We're not alone. You've got your witnesses."

"You bet I have. I'll probably have more when I'm talking to the attorney general. I'm going to tell him how you tried to buy Papps—buy him with cash, your stockholders' cash. How you finally swung Leeson and had him eating out of your hand. How you got him to arrange this little fishing party, here at your place, so you'd have Kelefy and Papps all to yourself. How Papps didn't like that and got me invited. And then after we got here, how I worked you into a corner with the dirty swindle you thought you had all set, and yesterday afternoon Leeson began to see the light. It didn't need much more to cook you good—one more day would have done it. This is the day. This is the day, but Leeson's not here. That's what I'm going to tell the attorney general, and I didn't want to spring it on you without warning. Also I didn't want you to claim I had, with a big whine, so I wanted witnesses. That's all."

Ferris turned and was going. Bragan called to him but he didn't stop. Bragan got up and made for him, but by the time he reached the door Ferris was through it, pulling it shut as he went. Bragan looked at me without seeing me, said, "By God, and he bought Papps himself!" and opened the door and was gone. I closed it and turned my back on it, and asked Wolfe, "Do I go and warn somebody? Or wait a while and then go find the body?"

"Pleistocene," he growled. "Saber-toothed hyenas."

"Okay," I agreed, "but all the same I think you missed a bet. That gook might actually be able to talk us out of here. If so, consider this. Driving time from here to Thirty-fifth Street, Manhattan, seven hours. Plane from here to Washington, three hours. I take a taxi to the city and start operating, and you hop a plane to New York. Flying to La Guardia, an hour and a quarter. Taxi from La Guardia to Thirty-fifth Street, forty-five minutes. Total traveling time, five hours. Two hours less than it would take to drive there, not to mention the fact that they won't let us. And in addition, bill Bragan for at least ten grand. You could tell him—"

"Archie."

"Yes, sir."

"There's a book on a shelf in that room—*Power and Policy*, by Thomas K. Finletter. I'd like to have it."

It had long been understood that at home he got his own books off of shelves, but I had to admit this was different, so I humored him. Going down the hall I kept my ears open for sounds of combat, but all was quiet. In the big room a trooper sat over by the door. I found the book with no trouble, and returned to Wolfe's room and handed it to him.

"It occurs to me," he said, "that a little later there'll probably be some fussing in the kitchen. They may even undertake to gather at a table for a meal. In the refrigerator are a third of a Ryder ham, half of a roast turkey, tree-ripened olives, milk, and beer. The bread is inedible, but in a cupboard there are some Caswell crackers, and in another cupboard a jar of Brantling's blackberry jam. If you see anything else you think desirable, bring it."

He opened the book and settled back in the chair. I wasn't through with him on the notion of letting Bragan spring us and commit himself to a fee, partly because I had a suspicion that Bragan's slant on the murder was the best bet in sight, but I thought half an hour with a book might make him more receptive to the idea of a plane ride, so I took to the hall again and on through to the kitchen. The cook, Samek, was there, with an array of dishes and trays and assorted grub scattered around. I said if he didn't mind I'd cater with a pair of trays for Wolfe and me, and he said go ahead. As I got out a bottle of milk I asked casually, "By the way, I intended to take a look at the trout the ambassador caught. Where are they?"

"They're not here. The cops took 'em."

The loaded trays called for two trips. The second trip, with mine, I met Papps in the hall and exchanged nods with him. Our meal, in Wolfe's room, went down all right, except that Wolfe drank beer with it, which he seldom does at home, and ruined his palate for the blackberry jam, so he said. I had had milk and my palate let the jam by without a murmur.

After returning the trays to the kitchen I headed back for the room, all set to tackle Wolfe on Bragan's proposition. My chances of selling him were about one in fifty, but I had to do something to pass the time and why not that? Keeping him stirred up was one thing he paid me for. However, it had to be postponed. As I approached I saw that the door was standing open, and as I entered I saw that we had more company. Adria Kelefy was sitting in the chair that I had moved up for Bragan, and the ambassador was getting another for himself, to make it a trio.

I closed the door.

## VII

I got snubbed again. As I stepped around to a chair off to one side, Wolfe and Mrs. Kelefy merely glanced at me, and the ambassador didn't even bother to glance. He was talking.

"I am well acquainted," he was saying, "with Finletter's theory that in the atomic age we can no longer rely on industrial potential as the dominant factor in another world war, and I think he makes his point, but he goes too far. In spite of that, it's a good book, a valuable book."

Wolfe placed a slip of paper in it to mark his place —he dog's-ears his own books—and put it down. "In any event," he said, "man is a remarkable animal, with a unique distinction. Of all the millions of species rendered extinct by evolution, we are the only one to know in advance what is going to destroy us. Our own insatiable curiosity. We can take pride in that."

"Yes indeed." Evidently Kelefy wasn't too upset at the prospect. "I had hoped, Mr. Wolfe, to offer you my thanks in happier circumstances. The death of Mr. Leeson has turned this little excursion into a tragedy, but even so, I must not neglect to thank you. It was most gracious of you to grant my request."

"It was a privilege and an honor," Wolfe declared. No diplomat was going to beat him at it. "To be chosen as an instrument of my country's hospitality was my good fortune. I only regret, with you, the catastrophe that spoiled it."

"Of course," the ambassador agreed. "I thought also to tell you how I happened to make the request of Secretary Leeson. There is a man who operates a restaurant in Rome, where I was once stationed, by the name of Pasquale Donofrio. I praised his sauce with grilled kidneys, and he said you originated it. I had a similar experience in Cairo, and one in Madrid. And from my friend Leeson, when he had a post in my own capital, I heard something of your exploits as a private detective. So when, here in your country, I was asked to express a personal desire, I thought of you."

"I am gratified, sir. I am lifted."

"And my wife joins me in my thanks." He smiled at her. "My dear?"

Her dark eyes were as sleepy as ever. Apparently it would take more than a murder to light them up. She spoke. "I insisted on coming with my husband to thank you, Mr. Wolfe. I too had heard much about you, and the trout was delicious. Really the best I have ever tasted. And another thing, I wanted to ask you, some more of our insatiable curiosity, why didn't you cook the ones my husband caught?"

"Oh yes," Kelefy agreed. "I wanted to ask that too."

"Caprice," Wolfe said. "Mr. Goodwin will tell you that I am a confirmed eccentric."

"Then you really cooked none of mine?"

"That seems to be established."

"But it's rather fantastic, since it was at my request that you were here. Even a caprice must spring from something."

"Not necessarily, sir." Wolfe was patient. "A whim, a fancy, a freakish dart of the mind."

The ambassador persisted. "I apologize for dwelling on this, but I would like to avoid any chance of embarrassment. Mr. Colvin made rather a point of it, probably in his eagerness to get at you, and it would be most unfortunate if it got into the public reports. In a *cause célèbre*, and this will certainly be one, any unexplained fact gives rise to all kinds of wild rumors, and in this instance they will concern me, only because it was the trout I caught that you didn't cook! It's true that that has no conceivable connection with the murder of Secretary Leeson, but the gossips will do their best to invent one, and the position of an ambassador is extremely delicate and sensitive, particularly mine at this moment. You know that, of course."

Wolfe nodded. "I do."

"Then you realize the difficulty. If you refuse to furnish any explanation, or if you only call it the caprice of an eccentric, what will be thought? What will not be thought?"

"Yes." Wolfe pursed his lips. "I see your point." He heaved a sigh. "Very well. It's not too hard a nut. I can say that my sense of humor is somewhat unorthodox, as indeed it is, and that it amuses me to twist the tails of highly placed persons; that since you had said you wanted to catch a trout and have it cooked by me, and I had traveled here for that express purpose, I thought it would be a nice touch of mockery not to cook any you had caught; and that with me to think is to act. Will that do?"

"Excellently. You will say that?"

"At the moment I see no objection to it. Some unforeseen contingency might of course provide one, so I can't make it a commitment."

"I wouldn't expect you to." He was unquestionably a diplomat. "And I must thank you again. There was another little matter—but am I imposing on you?"

"Not at all. Like the others, I am merely waiting for the arrival of the attorney general."

"Then I'll mention it briefly. Mr. Ferris has told me of his conversation with Mr. Bragan in your presence. He told me of it, he said, because my name came into it and it concerned my mission to this country. I told him that I deeply appreciated his telling me, and I also expressed a hope that he would abandon his intention of repeating it to the attorney general. We discussed the matter at some length, and in the end he agreed with me that his intention was ill-advised—that it would be greatly prejudicial to the negotiations in which we are both interested. He regretted the hot impulse that led him to come to you, and, finding Mr. Bragan here, to proceed as he did. He now feels compunction. It is not an exaggeration to say that he is in some despair because he thinks he has compromised himself by speaking to Mr. Bragan before witnesses, and he thinks it would be futile to come now and ask you and Mr. Goodwin to erase the episode from your memories. I told him it is never futile to ask honorable men to do an honorable thing, and that I would ask you myself. I do so. Believe me, it will serve no useful purpose for Mr. Ferris's outburst to Mr. Bragan to be repeated to anyone anywhere."

Wolfe grunted. "I do believe you. On this the commitment can be as firm as you like." He turned. "Archie?"

"Yes, sir."

"We remember nothing of what Mr. Ferris said to Mr. Bragan this afternoon, and no provocation by anyone will refresh our memory. You agree to that?"

"Yes, sir."

"Our honor has been invoked. On your word of honor?"

"Check. On my word of honor."

He turned. "And mine, sir. Is that adequate?"

"It is indeed." Kelefy said it as if he meant it. "Mr. Ferris will be delighted. As for me, I cannot properly express my appreciation, but I hope you will permit me to proffer a slight token of it." He lifted his left hand, and with the fingers of his right one began working at the ring with the emerald. It was a little stubborn, but after some twisting and tugging he got it off. He rubbed it on the sleeve of his jacket, and turned to his wife.

"I think, my dear," he said, "it would be fitting for you to present this to Mr. Wolfe. You wanted to come with me to thank him, and this is the symbol of our gratitude. Please beg him to accept it."

She seemed to hesitate a second, and I wondered if she had cottoned to my suggestion of an earring and hated to give it up. Then she took it without looking at it and extended her hand to Wolfe. "I do beg you to accept it," she said, in so low a voice that I barely caught it. "As a symbol of our gratitude."

Wolfe didn't hesitate. He took it, looked at it, and

closed his fingers over it. I expected him to do it up brown, to come out with something really flowery, but he surprised me again, which wasn't surprising. "This is quite unnecessary, madam," he told her. He turned. "Quite unnecessary, sir."

Kelefy was on his feet. He smiled. "If it were necessary it wouldn't be so great a pleasure. I must go and see Mr. Ferris. Thank you again, Mr. Wolfe. Come, my dear."

I went and opened the door for them. They passed through, with friendly glances for me but no emeralds, and I shut the door and crossed to Wolfe. The light from the windows, which were some distance from him, had started to fade, and he had turned on the reading lamp by his chair and was admiring the emerald under it. I admired it too. It was the size of a hazel nut.

"My word of honor may not be as good as yours," I said, "but it has some value. You wear it Monday to Friday, and I'll wear it Saturday and Sunday."

He grunted. "You brought your working case in, didn't you?"

"Yes. My gun's in it."

"I want the best glass, please."

I went to my room and unlocked the case and got the glass and returned. With it he gave the emerald a real look and then handed them to me. That seemed to imply that I had an equity, so I inspected the green symbol of gratitude from the front, back, and all sides.

"I'm not an expert," I said, returning it to him, "and it may be that little brown speck near the center adds to its rarity and beauty, but if I were you I'd give it back to him and ask for a nice clear one like some I saw not long ago in a window at Woolworth's."

No comment. I went to my room to return the

glass to my working case. If I was going to try to sell him on Bragan's offer I'd have to step on it, for time was closing in. I had my opening gun ready to fire as I re-entered his room, but after a couple of steps toward him I stopped dead. He was leaning back in the chair with his eyes closed, and his lips were working. He pushed them out, pulled them back in . . . push . . . pull . . . push . . . pull . . .

I stood and stared at him. He did that only when his brain was going full tilt, with all the wheels whirling and all the wires singing What now? What about? I couldn't suspect him of faking because that was the one phenomenon I had never seen him use for putting on an act. When his eyes were closed and his lips were moving like that he was really working, and working hard But on what? No client, no evidence, no itch whatever except to get in the car and start home. However, it was well established that when that fit took him he was not to be interrupted on any account, so I went to a window for another look out. The trooper was still on post, with his back to me. The sun had gone behind the trees, maybe even below the rim, and dusk was coming on. I couldn't see the light going if I kept my eyes on one spot, but I could if I kept them there for thirty seconds, then shifted to another spot for thirty seconds, and then back again. I had caught on to that out in Ohio about the time I was catching my first shiner.

Wolfe's voice turned me around. "What time is it?"

I glanced at my wrist. "Twenty minutes to eight."

He had straightened up and was stretching his eyes open. "I want to make a phone call. Where?"

"There's one in the big room, as you know. There must be extensions, surely one in Bragan's room, but I haven't seen any. I understand that phone calls are

being permitted, but they're monitored. There's a cop
in the big room, and not only that, you can bet they've
tapped the line outside."

"I must phone. It's essential." He put his hands on
the chair arms and levered himself up. "What is Nathaniel Parker's home number?"

"Lincoln three four-six-one-six."

"Come on." He headed for the door.

I followed him down the hall and into the big room.
The trooper was there, going around switching lamps
on. He gave us a glance but no words. On the table
with the phone there was a tray with an empty plate
and coffee cup, so apparently he had been foddered.
When Wolfe picked up the phone he moved in our
direction, but uttered no protest and didn't draw his
gun. Wolfe had taken out his notebook and opened it
on the table, and from across the table the trooper
focused on it, but all he saw was a blank page.

Wolfe was speaking: "Person-to-person call to a
New York City number. This is Whiteface seven-
eight-oh-eight. My name is Nero Wolfe. I wish to
speak to Mr. Nathaniel Parker in New York, at Lincoln three four-six-one-six."

I thought the trooper looked as if he would enjoy a
bone, so I told him, "Parker's our lawyer. A reputable
member of the bar and a very fine man. He's got me
out of jail three times."

He was in no humor for conversation. He stood. I
stood. At that time of evening it didn't take long for
the call to get through, and soon Wolfe was telling the
receiver, "Mr. Parker? . . . Yes, Nero Wolfe. I hope I
didn't interrupt your dinner. . . . I'm calling from
Mr. Bragan's lodge in the Adirondacks. . . . Yes, of
course you've heard. . . . I need some information

from you, *mais il faut parler français exclusivement. Vous comprenez? . . . Bien. . . .*"

He went on. The trooper was up against it. The phone calls were probably being recorded out at the tap, but no doubt he was supposed to stand by and note the substance, and he couldn't note meaningless sounds. The changes on his face kept me informed. First, he didn't know French, that was obvious. Next, he had an impulse to reach and cut the connection—he even started a hand out—but voted it down. Next, he tried looking intelligent and superior, indicating that he understood it perfectly, but gave it up when he glanced at me and met my eye. Next, he decided to pretend that there was no problem involved at all, that he was standing there only to see that Wolfe didn't twist the phone cord. Going through all the phases took a lot of time, a quarter of an hour or more, and he was doing pretty well with the last one when Wolfe did him a favor by getting out his pencil and starting to write in the notebook. That gave the cop something to look at, and was a big relief to both of us, though I doubted if he could read Wolfe's fine small handwriting upside down at a distance of five feet. I was closer, and, stretching my neck, saw that he was writing the same lingo he was speaking. Since I don't know French either, I just looked intelligent.

Wolfe filled a page of the notebook and part of another, and then suddenly went back to English. "Thank you very much, Mr. Parker. Satisfactory. I apologize for interrupting your dinner, but it was urgent. . . . No, I have nothing to add and nothing more to ask. . . . Yes, I shall, but I doubt if I'll need you again. Good-by, sir."

He hung up, put the notebook in his pocket, turned to me, and opened his mouth to speak, but didn't get it out. The door to the veranda swung open and people entered—first District Attorney Colvin, then a medium-sized guy with a round red face and big ears, and last Sheriff Dell.

Colvin, seeing us, stopped and turned. "That's Nero Wolfe. Wolfe and Goodwin." He came on. "Wolfe, this is Mr. Herman Jessel, attorney general of the state of New York. I've told him how things stand, and he'll talk with you first. Now."

"Excellent," Wolfe declared. "I'm ready, and it shouldn't take long. But not privately. If I am to disclose the murderer of Mr. Leeson, as I now intend, it must be in the presence of everyone concerned. If you'll please have them gathered here?"

They goggled at him. The sheriff said something. Colvin's specs slipped to the tip of his nose, but he ignored them.

Jessel was confronting Wolfe. "Will you repeat that, please?"

"It was clear, I thought. I am prepared to identify the murderer. I will do so only in the presence of the others. I will say nothing whatever, answer no questions, except with them present. And when they are here, all of them, and of course you gentlemen too, I must first speak to the Secretary of State on the telephone. If he is not in Washington he must be located. I assure you, gentlemen, it is useless to start barking at me or haul me off somewhere; I'll be mute. There is no acceptable way to proceed other than the one I suggested."

The sheriff and the DA looked at each other. Jessel looked at Wolfe. "I've met you once before, Mr. Wolfe. You've probably forgotten."

"No, sir, I haven't."

"And I know your record, of course. You say you can identify the murderer. With evidence?"

"To convict, no. To indict, yes. To convince all who hear me, including you, beyond question."

"What's this about the Secretary of State?"

"I must begin by speaking to him. The reason will be apparent when you hear me."

"All right. We can reach him. But I have a must too. I must first hear from you privately what you're going to say."

"No, sir." Wolfe's tone was final. "Not a word."

"Why not?"

"Because I have a score to pay, and if I told you first you might somehow interfere with the payment." Wolfe turned a palm up. "What is so difficult? Get them in here. Get the Secretary of State on the phone. I speak to him. You can stop me at any point, at any word. Stand beside me, ready to snatch it from me. Station a policeman behind me with a club."

"I'll take it as a great personal favor if you'll talk with me first."

Wolfe shook his head. "I'm sorry, Mr. Jessel. I'm far too pigheaded. Give it up."

The attorney general looked around. If for suggestions, he got none. He shoved his hands in his pockets, wheeled, and walked toward the fireplace. Halfway there he turned abruptly and came back, and asked Colvin, "They're all here?"

"Yes, certainly."

"Send for them, please. I'll put in the call."

Attorney General Jessel, standing, was speaking into the phone. "Then you understand the situation, Mr. Secretary. One moment. Here is Mr. Wolfe."

He handed the instrument to Wolfe, who was seated. Bragan and the ambassador and Mrs. Kelefy were on a divan that had been turned around. Mrs. Leeson was on a chair at the end of the divan. Spiros Papps, the man of guile and malice and simple candor, was perched on a big fat cushion in front of Mrs. Leeson. Ferris and the sheriff had chairs a little to one side, with Lieutenant Hopp and two of his colleagues standing back of them. District Attorney Colvin stood by the table, practically at Wolfe's elbow, and Jessel, after handing Wolfe the phone, stayed there at the other elbow. I was on my feet too, at Wolfe's back. I hadn't a glimmer of an idea where he was headed for, but he had said he was going to identify a murderer, so while they were arranging things I had gone to my room, got my gun, and put it in my side pocket.

Wolfe's tone was easy. "This is Nero Wolfe, Mr. Secretary. I should have asked Mr. Jessel to say that this will take some time, ten minutes or more, I'm afraid, so I trust you are comfortably seated. . . . Yes sir, I know; I won't prolong it beyond necessity. You already know the details of the situation, so I'll go straight to my personal predicament. I know who killed Mr. Leeson. It would be pointless to denounce him to officers of the law. But I want to denounce him; first, because if I don't I'll be detained and harassed here interminably; and second, because he has foolishly wounded my self-esteem. . . . Yes sir, but if I tell it at all I have to tell it my way, and I think you should hear it first. . . .

"Today I was to cook trout for lunch. Four creels, tagged with the names of the fishermen, were brought to me. The fish in three of the creels were perfectly fresh and sweet, but those in Ambassador Kelefy's creel were not. They were not stiff or discolored, nothing so obvious; indeed, the cook apparently saw nothing wrong with them; but they had not been caught this morning. It would take too long to explain how an expert tells exactly how long a fish has been dead no matter how carefully it has been handled, but I assure you I can do it infallibly. Of course I decided not to include them in my dish. The cook asked why, but I didn't explain, not wishing to embarrass the ambassador. Naturally, I supposed either his luck or his skill had failed him this morning, and he had somehow procured those dead trout to cover his deficiency.

"I am making this as brief as I can. The news of Mr. Leeson's death by violence put a different face on the matter. The inescapable presumption was that Ambassador Kelefy had killed him, and it was indeed premeditated. He had caught those eight trout yesterday in addition to what he brought in—I haven't bothered to inquire about that—and had secured them at the edge of a pool in the river, immersed in the water. Probably they were alive when he did that, but I am not sufficiently expert to name the precise hour when they died. Also he probably secured his weapon from the woodpile yesterday and hid it somewhere. So today, having to spend no time fishing in order to bring in a satisfactory creel, he had four hours for another matter—the murder of Mr. Leeson.

Getting through the woods unobserved presented no difficulty.

"That was my presumption, but I would have been an ass to disclose it. It was only a presumption, and I was the only witness of the condition of the trout in his creel. Officers of the law have examined them without seeing what I did—though in fairness it must be considered that when I saw them they were supposed to have just come from freedom in the river, and the officers saw them some four hours later. Even so, when the district attorney asked me why I had not cooked the ambassador's trout I might have told him, privately, but for his gratuitous spleen.

"Now, however, it is more than a presumption. The ambassador has not explicitly confessed to me, but he might as well have. A little more than an hour ago he came to my room, with his wife, ostensibly to thank me, and asked why I had not cooked the trout he caught. From my reply, and the sequel, he understood what was in my mind. At his suggestion I concocted a bogus explanation. He asked me to commit myself to it, and I straddled. He then made another request, no matter what, which he knew quite well to be unnecessary, since we understood each other tacitly or he thought we did, and when I granted it freely without hesitation he offered me a token of his gratitude by taking an emerald ring from his finger and telling his wife to present it to me. She did so, and it is now in my vest pocket.

"That, Mr. Secretary, was the wound to my self-esteem. The emerald was not a token of gratitude for anything I had done; it was a bribe to keep my mouth shut. Had it measured up to my conceit—had it been the Kohinoor or the Zabara—it might have served its purpose; but it is merely a rather large emerald with a noticeable flaw. So naturally I was piqued. When the ambassador left me I sat and considered the matter. Not only was I piqued, I was menaced, and so were others. Unless the ambassador were exposed we would suffer prolonged harassment and probably life-long suspicion, and only I could expose him. I decided I must act, but first I needed to know what was feasible and what was not, so I telephoned my lawyer in New York.

"From books in his library he supplied the information I wanted, and I wrote it in my notebook. To make this report complete I must read it to you.

*"From Section Twenty-five of the Penal Code of New York State: 'Ambassadors and other public ministers from foreign governments, accredited to the President or Government of the United States, and recognized according to the laws of the United States, with their secretaries, messengers, families, and servants, are not liable to punishment in this State, but are to be returned to their own country for trial and punishment.'*

*"From Section Two-fifty-two of Title Twenty-two of the United States Code: 'Whenever any writ or process is sued out or prosecuted by any person in any court of the United States, or of a State, or by any judge or justice, whereby the person of any ambassador or public minister of any foreign prince or state, authorized and received as such by the President, or any domestic or domestic servant of any such minister, is arrested or imprisoned, or his goods or chattels are distrained, seized, or at-*

*tached, such writ or process shall be deemed void.'*

"*From Section Two-fifty-three—I'll condense this: 'Anyone who obtains a writ or process in violation of Section Two-fifty-two, and every officer concerned in executing such writ or process, shall be deemed a violator of the law of nations and a disturber of the public repose, and shall be imprisoned for not more than three years and shall be fined at the discretion of the court.'*"

"That last, Mr. Secretary, explains why I insisted on speaking to you. If I had reported to the officers of the law who are here, and if in their zeal for justice they had maltreated the ambassador, not only would they have been subject to prosecution under federal law, but so would I. I don't want to be imprisoned for three years, or even to risk any hazard of it, and I chose the expedient of reporting directly to you. I am of course leaving one question unanswered: What was his motive? Why did he kill? I haven't the answer, but I do have a conjecture. You will like to know, I think, that it is unlikely that his motive had any relation to his public mission or the negotiations he was engaged in.

"As I told you, he didn't give me the emerald himself; he had his wife present it. His exact words were, 'I think, my dear, it would be fitting for you to present this to Mr. Wolfe,' and not only were the words suggestive, but so were his tone and manner. He was giving me the emerald as a bribe not to divulge my surmise that he had murdered Mr. Leeson. Then why was it fitting for his wife to present it to me? Because she had herself been involved? Because she had supplied either the impulse or the motive? Because, in short, she was responsible for his having resorted to the extremity—"

So it was Wolfe, not I, who found out what it took to light up Adria Kelefy's eyes. She came off the couch and through the air like a wildcat, and with a sweep of her hand knocked the phone, the whole works, off the table onto the floor. Colvin and Jessel dived for the phone. I took on the wildcat, grabbing her arms from behind, and she tugged and twisted and kicked my shins. Jessel got the phone and was telling it hello hello hello, when another voice broke in.

"Yes, she was responsible." It was Sally Leeson. She had left her chair and circled around Papps to come within arm's length of Adria Kelefy. I tightened up on Adria's arms. Sally went on, in an even, dead, flat tone that froze the air and all of us breathing it. "You're not even a snake, Adria. I don't know what you are. You seduced my husband in your own home, your husband's home. I knew about it. He told me he couldn't tear away from you, so I tore him away and got him called back home. I suppose you told your husband about it—I think you would. After we had left, I suppose, in one of your big fits. Then he was sent over here, and the day you got here you were after my husband again. I knew it and I tried to stop you, and I failed. Your husband hasn't failed. He has succeeded. He killed Dave. Why didn't he kill you?" She tightened her fists, hanging at her sides, stiffened, and then started to tremble. "Oh God," she cried, "why didn't he kill you?"

She stopped trembling, turned to the district attorney, and was stiff again. "I told you a lie," she said. "When I said I didn't suspect anyone. Of course I did.

But I knew you couldn't arrest him—and I didn't want to tell you what a fool my husband had been—and what good would it do? What good will anything do now?" She started to tremble again.

The ambassador had left the couch to come to us, and for a second I thought he was actually going to answer her. But he spoke, not to her, but to his wife. He put a hand on Adria's shoulder, and I stepped back. "Come, my dear," he said. "This is distressing." She moved, and he turned his head and called sharply, "Spiros!"

That was a sight I had never expected to see and don't expect to see again. Standing there were an attorney general, a district attorney, a sheriff, and three state troopers in uniform, not to mention, a pair of private detectives; and none of them moved a muscle while a murderer calmly walked out of the room, taking with him his wife, who had driven him to murder, and a member of his staff, who had certainly known he was guilty.

But Wolfe moved his jaw muscles. He spoke sharply to their backs. "Mr. Kelefy! If you please. A purely personal point. Was it also a stab at my self-esteem that you arranged for me to be here? For the added fillip of gulling me?"

"No, Mr. Wolfe." The ambassador had turned at the door. "When I expressed a desire to eat a trout cooked by you I had not yet contemplated an action that might arouse your professional interest. I had not forgotten the past, but I had accepted it. When events caused me to contemplate such an action it would have been imprudent, I thought, to ask you not to come."

Turning, he touched his wife's elbow and they disappeared into the hall, with Spiros Papps at their heels.

The tableau broke up. Jessel muttered something about the Secretary of State and went at the phone. Colvin pushed his specs back. The sheriff and the lieutenant exchanged words. The troopers stood looking dazed.

Wolfe, on his feet, took the emerald ring from his pocket and handed it to the DA. "Dispose of this as you see fit, Mr. Colvin. You were right about the notable incident, of course. Mr. Goodwin and I will be packed and ready to go in five minutes. If you will kindly pass the word? Come, Archie."

He headed for the hall and I followed.

## IX

Of course you would like to know if Kelefy paid for it, and so would I. He left for home the next day, taking his wife and Papps along, and a month later they shot him, but whether it was for the murder or for ruining the negotiations I can't say. Diplomatically speaking, I doubt if he cared much.

# Too Many
# Detectives

# I

I am against female detectives on principle. It's not always and everywhere a tough game, but most of the time it is, with no room for the friendly feelings and the nice little impulses. So a she-dick must have a good thick hide, which is not a skin I'd love to touch; if she hasn't, she is apt to melt just when a cold eye and hard nerves are called for, and in that case she doesn't belong.

However, there are times when a principle should take a nap, and that was one of them. Of the seven private detectives present in the room, including Nero Wolfe and me, two were women, seated in a corner, side by side. Theodolinda (Dol) Bonner, about my age, with home-grown long black lashes making a curling canopy for her caramel-colored eyes, had had her own agency as a licensed detective for some years and was doing all right. She might have got her well-cut and well-hung brown tweed suit at Bergdorf's and possibly the mink jacket too. I had seen her before, but I knew the name of the other one, Sally Colt, only because the members of the little gathering had exchanged names and greetings at the suggestion of Jay Kerr.

I left my chair, crossed to the corner, got upturned eyes, and spoke. "Miss Colt? I don't know if you caught my name. Archie Goodwin."

"Yes, of course," she said. Her skin didn't look thick, and her voice didn't sound thick. She was the right age to be my younger sister, but I didn't particularly need a sister. Her woolen dress and camel's-hair coat hadn't come from Bergdorf's, but I didn't at all need duds from Bergdorf's.

I looked at my wrist and back at her. "It's a quarter past eleven," I told her, "and there's no telling how much longer they'll keep us waiting. I saw a counter downstairs, and I'll go get coffee for the bunch if you'll come and help carry. Couldn't you use some coffee, Miss Bonner?"

Miss Colt looked at Miss Bonner, her employer, and Miss Bonner nodded at her and then told me it was a fine idea. I turned and raised my voice to ask if anyone didn't want coffee, and got no turndowns, and Sally Colt got up and we left.

I was perfectly willing to drink some coffee. Also the physical aspects and carriage of Miss Colt had given me the impression that there might be some flaw in my attitude toward female detectives, and I wanted to check on it. But chiefly I wanted a little recess from the sight of Nero Wolfe's mug, which I had never seen quite so sour, and the fact that he had had plenty of provocation didn't make him any prettier. It was a very sad story. The wiretapping scandals had called attention to various details concerning private detectives, to wit, that there were 590 of them licensed by the secretary of state of the state of New York; that 432 of the 590 were in New York City; that applicants for licenses took no written examination and no formal inquiry was made into their backgrounds; that the State Department had no idea how many operatives were employed by the licensed detectives, since the employees weren't licensed at all; and a lot of so on and so forth.

So the secretary of state decided to inquire, and all of the 590 were summoned to appear for questioning, specifically about wiretapping activities, if any, and generally about the whole setup. Wolfe and I both had licenses and were therefore both summoned, and of course that was a nuisance, but since it was being shared by the other 588 he might have kept his reaction down to a few dozen growls and grumbles if it hadn't been for two things. First, the inquiry was being held partly in New York and partly in Albany, and we had been summoned to Albany, and his request to get it changed to New York had been ignored; and second, the only wiretapping operation he had ever had a hand in had added nothing to his glory and damn little to his bank account, and he didn't want to be reminded of it.

So when, in Wolfe's old brownstone house, at five o'clock that winter morning, Fritz had taken his breakfast up to his room, and I had gone along to tell him the weather was possible for driving and he wouldn't have to risk the perils of a train, he was too sunk in gloom even to growl. All the way to Albany, 160 miles and four hours, with him in the back seat of the sedan as usual so he wouldn't go through the windshield when we crashed, he uttered maybe twenty words, none of them affable, and when I called his attention to the attractions of the new Thruway, which he had not seen before, he shut his eyes. We had arrived at the building in Albany to which we had been summoned at 9:55, five minutes earlier than specified, and had been directed to a room on the third floor and told to wait. There had of course been no chair adequate for his massive bulk. He had glanced around, stood a moment, croaked "Good morning" to those already there, gone to a chair at the far wall and got himself lowered, and sat and sulked for an hour and a quarter.

I must admit that the five others weren't very festive either. When Jay Kerr decided it ought to be more sociable he did get names passed around, but that was about all, though we were fellow members of ALPDNYS, the Association of Licensed Private Detectives of New York State—except, of course, Sally Colt, who was merely an employed operative. Jay Kerr, a half-bald roly-poly with rimless cheaters, was probably trying to even up a little by making an effort to get people together, since he had helped to get so many apart. He and his boys had tailed more husbands for wives and wives for husbands than any other outfit in the metropolitan area. Harland Ide, tall and bony, gray at the temples, with a long hawk's nose, dressed like a banker, was well known in the trade too, but with a difference. He was an old pro with a reputation for high standards, and it was said that he had more than once been called in for consultation by the FBI, but don't quote me. I wasn't up on the third one, Steve Amsel, having heard only a few casual remarks about him here and there when he got the boot from Larry Bascom a couple of years back and got himself a license and rented a midtown room. Bascom, who runs one of the best agencies in town, had told someone that Amsel wasn't a lone eagle, he was a lone buzzard. He was small and dark and very neat, with quick black eyes that kept darting around looking for a place to light, and he probably wasn't as young as he looked. When Sally Colt and I went to get coffee he left his chair and was going to offer to come along, but decided not to.

At the counter downstairs, while we were waiting for the coffee, I told Sally not to worry. "If you and your boss get hooked for a tapping job, just give Mr. Wolfe a ring and he'll refer it to me and I'll fix it. No charge. Professional courtesy."

"Now that's sweet." She had her head tilted, for me to have the best angle on the line from under her ear to her chin, which was good. Showing that she was not only an attractive girl, but also kind-hearted, thinking of others. "I'll match you. When you and your boss get hooked, give Miss Bonner a ring. My boss can lick your boss."

"That's the spirit," I approved. "Loyalty or bust. You'll get pie in the sky when you die. I suppose your personal specialty is getting the subject in a corner in Peacock Alley and charming it out of him. If you ever feel like practicing on me I might consider it, only I don't charm very easy."

She straightened her head to meet eye to eye. Hers were dark blue. "You might be a little tough, at that," she said. "It might take a full hour to break you wide open."

The coffee came and interrupted. By the time we got to the elevator I had a return ready, a crusher, but there was company and I had to save it, and back in the room with our colleagues was no good either. She served Nero Wolfe first and I served Dol Bonner. After the others had been attended to I joined the ladies in their corner, but I didn't want to demolish Sally in front of her boss, so we merely discussed how much longer we might have to wait. That was soon decided—for me, anyhow. There was still coffee in my container when a man entered and announced that

Nero Wolfe and Archie Goodwin were wanted. Wolfe heaved a sigh for all to hear, put his container down on a chair, arose, and headed for the door, and I followed, as a murmur went around. The man led us twenty paces down the hall, opened a door and went in, and fingered to us to enter. The staff of the secretary of state needed training in manners.

It was a medium-sized room with three large windows, all weather-dirty. In the center was a big walnut table surrounded by chairs, and against the walls were a desk and a smaller table and more chairs. A man seated at one end of the big table, with a stack of folders at his right, motioned us to chairs at his left. The one who had brought us closed the door and took a nearby chair against the wall.

The man at the table gave us a look, neither cordial nor hostile. "I guess there's no question of identity with you," he told Wolfe, meaning either that he was famous or that no one else was so big and fat, take your pick. He glanced at a folder open before him on the table. "I have your statements here, yours and Mr. Goodwin's. I thought it would expedite matters to have you in together. I am Albert Hyatt, special deputy of the secretary of state for this inquiry. The proceeding is informal and will remain so unless circumstances arise that seem to call for a record."

I was taking him in. Not far from forty, one way or the other, he was smooth all over—smooth healthy skin, smooth dark hair, smooth pleasant voice, smooth brisk manner, and smooth gray gabardine. I had of course checked on the two deputies who were handling the inquiry and had reported to Wolfe that this Hyatt was a partner in a big law firm with offices in midtown New York, that he had mixed a good deal in politics, that he had some reputation as a trial man, which meant that he liked to ask people questions, and that he was a bachelor.

He glanced at the folder again. "In April of last year, nineteen-fifty-five, you arranged for a tap on the private telephone of Otis Ross, at his apartment on West Eighty-third Street, Manhattan, New York City. Is that correct?"

"I have so stated," Wolfe conceded grumpily.

"So you have. Under what circumstances did you make that arrangement?"

Wolfe moved a finger to aim it at the folder. "If that's my statement before you, and Mr. Goodwin's, you have it there."

"Yes, I have your statement, but I'd like to hear it. Please answer the question."

Wolfe started to make a face, realized it wouldn't help matters any, and suppressed it. "On April fifth, nineteen-fifty-five, a man called on me at my office, gave his name as Otis Ross, and said he wanted to have his home telephone tapped. I told him I never dealt with marital difficulties. He said that his difficulty wasn't marital, that he was a widower, that he had diversified business and financial interests and handled them from his home, that he had recently begun to suspect his secretary of double dealing, that he was away frequently for a day or two at a time, that he wanted to find out whether his suspicions of his secretary were warranted, and to that end he wanted his phone tapped."

Wolfe tightened his lips. He hated to be reminded of that affair, let alone retell it. For a second I thought he was going to balk, but he went on. "I knew, of course, that it was legally permissible for a man to have his own wire tapped, but I declined the job on the ground that I had had no experience in that line.

Mr. Goodwin, who was present, as he always is at conversations in my office, interposed to say that he knew of a man who could handle the technical problem. He so interposed for two reasons: first, because of the novelty and diversion a wiretapping operation would offer him personally; and second, because he thinks it necessary to badger me into earning fees by taking jobs which I would prefer to reject. I confess that he is sometimes justified. Would you like him to interpose now for corroboration?"

Hyatt shook his head. "When you're through. Go ahead."

"Very well. Mr. Ross put a thousand dollars in cash on my desk—ten hundred-dollar bills—as a retainer and advance for expenses. He said he couldn't pay by check because his secretary must not know he had hired me, and also, for the same reason, no reports or other matter could be mailed to him; he would call for them at my office or make other arrangements to get them. And I was not to phone him at his home because he suspected that his secretary, on occasion, impersonated him on the telephone. Therefore he wanted reports of all conversations on his wire, since when he himself was presumed to be speaking at his end it might actually be his secretary."

Wolfe tightened his lips again. He was having to squeeze it out. "Naturally not only had my curiosity been aroused, but also my suspicions. It would have been useless to ask him for documentary evidence of his identity, since documents can be forged or stolen, so I told him that I must be satisfied of his bona fides, and I suggested that Mr. Goodwin might call on him at his home. You don't need to tell me how witless that suggestion was; I have told myself. He acquiesced at once, having, of course, anticipated it, saying only that it should be at an hour when his secretary would not be on the premises, since he—that is, his secretary—might possibly recognize Mr. Goodwin. So it was arranged. At nine o'clock that evening Mr. Goodwin went to the address on West Eighty-third Street and up to Mr. Ross's apartment. He gave the maid who admitted him a name—an alias that had been agreed upon—and asked to see Mr. Ross, and was taken by her to the living room, where he found my client seated under a lamp, reading a book and smoking a cigar."

Wolfe tapped the table with a fingertip. "I designate him 'my client' deliberately because I earned the ignominy—confound it, he *was* my client! After Mr. Goodwin conversed with him ten minutes or so he came home and reported, and it was decided to proceed with the operation. Mr. Goodwin got in touch with the man he knew of that evening, and arrangements were made for the morrow. Do you want the details of that?"

"No, you can skip that." Hyatt passed a palm over his smooth dark hair. "It's in Goodwin's statement."

"I know very little about it anyway. The tap was made, and Mr. Goodwin had a new toy. He couldn't spend much time with it, since I need him at the office more or less continually, and most of the listening was done by men provided by the technician. I didn't even look at the reports, for which Mr. Ross called at my office every day—at an hour when I was busy upstairs, so I didn't see him. On the fifth day Mr. Goodwin asked him for another thousand dollars, and got it, in cash. That left very little for me after paying the cost of the outside tap and maintaining surveillance. You know what an outside tap is?"

"Certainly. Practically all illegal taps are outside jobs."

"That may be." Wolfe upturned a palm. "But I didn't know this was illegal until the eighth day of the operation. On April thirteenth Mr. Goodwin spent two hours at the place where the tap was being monitored, and heard Mr. Ross himself on the wire in a long conversation. Whether it was actually Mr. Ross or was his secretary impersonating him, it sounded sufficiently unlike our client to arouse Mr. Goodwin's interest. From reports he had read and passed on to our client he had gathered a good deal of information about Mr. Ross's interests and activities—for example, that he had recently been appointed chairman of the Charity Funds Investigating Committee by the governor. He left and went to a phone booth, called Mr. Ross, got the same voice, told him he was a newspaper reporter, from the *Gazette*, made an appointment, went to the West Eighty-third Street address, and saw him and talked with him. He also saw the secretary. Neither of them was our client. I had been flummoxed."

Wolfe swallowed bile. "Utterly flummoxed," he said bitterly. "Mr. Goodwin came home and reported to me, and we considered the situation. We decided to wait until the client came that afternoon, at five-thirty as usual, for the daily report—though of course we canceled the tap at once. It seemed likely that there would be no alternative to turning him over to the police, with a full account of my fatuity, but I couldn't do that until I got my hands on him."

Wolfe swallowed again. "And he didn't come. I don't know why. Whether he had learned somehow either that we had canceled the tap, or that Mr. Goodwin had called on Mr. Ross—but speculation is bootless. He didn't come. He never did come. For a month most of Mr. Goodwin's time, for which I pay, was spent in trying to find him, without success, and Mr. Goodwin is a highly competent and ingenious man. Nor could he find the maid who had admitted him to the apartment. After a week had passed with no result I made an appointment to call on Mr. Ross at his home, and did so, and told him all about it. He was ruffled, naturally, but after some discussion he agreed that there was no point in informing the authorities until and unless I found the culprit. Mr. Goodwin was with me, and together we gave him an exhaustive description of our client, but he was unable to identify him. As for the maid, she had been with him only a short time, had left without notice, and he knew nothing about her."

Wolfe stopped, sighed deep, and let it out. "There it is. After a month Mr. Goodwin could no longer spend all his time on it, since he had other duties, but he has by no means forgotten that client and neither have I. We never will."

"I suppose not." Hyatt was smiling. "I may as well tell you, Mr. Wolfe, that personally I credit your story."

"Yes, sir. You may."

"I hope so. But of course you realize its weakness. No one but you and Mr. Goodwin ever saw this client of yours. No one else has any knowledge of what passed between you, and you can't find him and can't identify him. Frankly, if you should be charged with illegal interception of communications, and if the district attorney proceeded against you and you came to trial, it's quite possible you would be convicted."

Wolfe's brows went up a sixteenth of an inch. "If that's a threat, what do you suggest? If it's merely a reproach, I have earned it and much more. Lecture me as you will."

"You deserve it," Hyatt agreed. He smiled again. "I would enjoy it, too, but I won't indulge myself. The fact is, I think I have a surprise for you, and I only wanted to get acquainted with you before I confronted you with it." His eyes went to the man seated against the wall. "Corwin, there's a man in room thirty-eight across the hall. Bring him in here."

Corwin got up and opened the door and went, leaving the door open. The sound came of his heavy footsteps in the hall, then of a door opening, then footsteps again, much fainter, then a brief silence, and then his voice calling, "Mr. Hyatt! Come here!"

It was more of a yelp than a call. It sounded as if somebody had him by the throat. So when Hyatt jumped up and headed for the door I moved too and followed him out and across the hall to an open door down a few steps, and into the room. I was at his elbow when he stopped beside Corwin at the far end of a table to look down at a man on the floor. The man was in no condition to return the look. He was on his back, with his legs nearly straight making a V, and was dressed all right, including a necktie, only the necktie wasn't under his shirt collar. It was knotted tight around the skin of his neck. Although his face was purple, his eyes popping, and his tongue sticking out, I recognized him at once. Corwin and Hyatt, staring down at him, probably didn't know I was there, and in a second I wasn't. Stepping out and back to the other room, where Wolfe sat at the table glowering, I told him, "It's a surprise all right. Our client's in there on the floor. Someone tied his necktie too tight and he's dead."

I had known, of course, that that bozo had sunk a blade right in the center of Wolfe's self-esteem, but I didn't realize how deep it had gone until that moment. Evidently when he heard me say our client was in there his ears stopped working. He came up out of his chair and took a step toward the door, then stopped, turned, and glared at me.

"Oh," he said, coming to. "Dead?"

"Right. Strangled."

"It would be no satisfaction to see him dead." He looked at the door, at me, sat down, flattened his palms on the table top, and closed his eyes. After a little he opened them. "Confound that wretch," he muttered. "Alive he gulled me, and now dead he gets me into heaven knows what. Perhaps if we went . . . but no. I am merely frantic." He stood up. "Come." He started for the door.

I got in front of him. "Hold it. I want to go home too, but you know damn well we can't scoot."

"I do indeed. But I want a look at our confreres. Come."

I stood aside and let him lead the way out and down the hall and into the room we had come from. Entering behind him, I shut the door. The two females were still in their corner, but the three men were gathered in a group, apparently having broken the ice. They all looked around at us, and Jay Kerr sang out, "What, still at large? How is he?"

Wolfe stood and took them in. So did I. At that point there was no particular reason to assume that one of them had tied our client's necktie, but the client had unquestionably been connected with wiretapping, and they had all been summoned to answer questions about wiretapping. So Wolfe and I took them in. None of them trembled or turned pale or licked his lips or had a fit.

Wolfe spoke. "Ladies and gentlemen, we are fellow members of a professional association, and therefore you might expect me to share with you any information I may have of our common concern. But I have just learned of an event in this building this morning that will cause Mr. Goodwin and me to suffer inconvenience and possibly serious harassment. I have no reason to suppose that any of you were involved in it, but you may have been; and if you weren't, you would gain nothing by hearing it from me, so I'll let someone else tell you about it. You won't have long to wait. Meanwhile, please understand that I mean no offense in staring around at you. I am merely interested in the possibility that one of you *is* involved. If you—"

"What the hell!" Steve Amsel snorted. His quick black eyes had lit at last. "You got a point?"

"It's a good script and I like it," Jay Kerr said. "Go right on." His voice was thin and high, but that was no sign that he had strangled a man. It was just his voice.

Harland Ide, the banker type, cleared his throat. "If we're not involved," he said drily, "we are not concerned. You say in this building this morning? What kind of an event?"

Wolfe shook his head, and stood and stared around. Still no one had a fit. Instead, they talked, and the general feeling seemed to be one of relief that they had been given something to talk about. Steve Amsel suggested that Dol Bonner and Sally Colt should get Wolfe between them and worm it out of him, but the ladies politely declined.

Wolfe was still standing, still taking them in, when the door popped open and Albert Hyatt appeared. Seeing Wolfe, he stopped short and said, "Oh, here you are." A strand of his smooth hair had got loose. He looked at me. "You too. You came in behind me and saw him, didn't you?"

I told him yes.

"And left in a hurry?"

"Sure. You had told Mr. Wolfe you had a surprise for him, and I wanted to tell him what it was."

"You recognized him?"

"I did. The client Mr. Wolfe told you about."

Wolfe put in, "I would have appreciated the favor of seeing him alive."

"Perhaps. Of course you have told these people?"

"No, sir."

"You haven't?"

"No."

Hyatt's eyes went around. "Apparently you're all here. Jay Kerr?"

"That's me," Kerr admitted.

"Harland Ide?"

"Here."

"Steven Amsel?"

Amsel raised a hand.

"Theodolinda Bonner?"

"I'm here, and I've been here more than two hours. I am quite willing to—"

"One moment, Miss Bonner. Sally Colt?"

"Here."

"All right. The hearing I am conducting on behalf of the secretary of state is temporarily suspended, but you will all stay in this room. A dead body has been discovered in a room on this floor. A man presumably murdered. That is of course a matter for the police, and they will want to see you. I can't say now when the hearing will be resumed, and you will regard your summonses to appear today as in abeyance but not canceled. Don't leave this room until the police come." He turned to go. A voice stopped him.

"Who is the murdered man?" It was Harland Ide.

"The police will tell you. That's not my province, thank God."

"Mr. Hyatt." Dol Bonner's voice was clear and crisp. She was on her feet. "You are Mr. Hyatt?"

"I am."

"Miss Colt and I had a very early breakfast, and we're hungry. We are going to get something to eat."

Damn plucky, I thought. She must have known that a murderer is supposed to feel empty and want a big meal after killing a man. Hyatt told her she'd have to wait until the police came, ignored a protest from Steve Amsel, and left, closing the door.

They looked around at one another. I was disappointed in them. I had on various occasions been cooped up with an assortment of people on account of a murder, but that was the first time they were exclusively private detectives, and you might have thought they would be a little quicker on the ball than most. No. It would have taken an average group maybe a minute to absorb the shock of Hyatt's announcement and hop on Wolfe and me, and that was about what it took them. Steve Amsel got to it first. He was about half Wolfe's size, and, facing him close, he had to tilt his head back to give his quick black eyes a straight line.

"So that was the event. Murder." He didn't make

it "moider" but something in between. "Okay. Who was it?"

Jay Kerr joined in. "Yeah, Goodwin recognized him. Name him."

Dol Bonner approached, expectantly, with Sally trailing behind her elbow. Harland Ide said, "If I heard correctly, Mr. Wolfe, he was a client of yours?"

They were hemming Wolfe in, and he backed up a step. "I can't tell you who he was," he said, "because I don't know. Neither does Mr. Goodwin. We don't know his name."

Sally Colt started to titter and choked it. "Nuts," Steve Amsel said, disgusted. "But Goodwin recognized him? This a guessing game you thought up?"

"And he was your client?" Jay Kerr squeaked.

"Really, Mr. Wolfe," Dol Bonner protested, "aren't you making a farce of it? You, with your reputation? Do you expect us to believe that you took a man as a client without even learning his name?"

"No." Wolfe compressed his lips. He released them. "Ladies and gentlemen, I am compelled to ask your forbearance. The silliest blunder I have ever made has found me here today, to my deep chagrin and possibly my undoing. What more do you want? What further ignominy? Mr. Goodwin recognized him, he was my client, I don't know his name, and before and after the period when I worked for him I know nothing whatever about him. That's all."

He marched to a chair against the wall, sat, rested his fists on his thighs, and closed his eyes.

I crossed over to him and lowered my voice. "Any instructions?"

"No." His eyes stayed shut.

"As you know, Gil Tauber is here in Albany. He

certainly knows the cops. Shall I go find a phone and alert him in case we could use some information?"

"No."

Evidently he didn't feel like chatting. I went over to the confreres, still in a group, and told them, "If you folks want to discuss our ignominy, don't mind me. You might even say something helpful."

"Where's the body?" Steve Amsel asked.

"Room thirty-eight, down the hall."

"What killed him?"

"His necktie around his throat. I suppose he could have done it himself, but you know how that is. I prefer not, and he might have been calmed down first with a heavy brass ashtray. There was one there on the floor."

"You and Wolfe came last this morning," Harland Ide stated. "Did you see him on the way?"

I grinned at him. "Now look," I objected. "We'll get enough of that from the cops. Have a heart. We're fellow members of a professional association. *You* would grill me?"

"Not at all," he said stiffly. "I merely thought that if that room is between here and the elevator, and the door was open, you might have seen him, possibly even spoken with him. I certainly did not intend—"

He was interrupted. The door opened and a man entered, a big broad-shouldered ape with not enough features to fill up his big round face. He shut the door, stood, and counted us, with his lips moving, and then pulled a chair over by the door and sat. He had nothing to say.

Again that bunch of pros disappointed me. They knew quite well that the presence of the dick had no bearing on their freedom to converse, and as for being discreet, one glance at his mug should have made it plain that he lacked the mental machinery to register and report anything he heard, granting he could hear. But they clammed up, and stayed clammed for a good half an hour. Just to see, I made a few tries at starting some discourse, but nothing doing. The ladies had gone back to their corner, and I tried them too, and got the impression that Sally would have been willing to relieve the tension with a little give and take, but as for Dol Bonner, definitely not, and she was the boss.

I had just glanced at my wrist watch and seen ten minutes past one when the door opened again. This time there were two of them. The one in front was a six-footer with a long narrow phiz and grizzled hair. He stopped three paces in, sent his eyes around, and told us, "I'm Leon Groom, chief of detectives of the City of Albany."

He paused, for applause maybe, but didn't get it. His facial expression was superior, and so was his tone of voice, which was natural under the circumstances. Not often does a chief of detectives get to address an audience composed exclusively of private eyes, a breed they would like to blackball, and not only that, we were all from the big town, which made us mud.

He resumed. "You have been told that there has been a death by violence in a room on this floor, and you're being detained for questioning. Nero Wolfe and Archie Goodwin will come with me. Now. The rest of you will shortly be taken, one at a time, to view the body." He aimed a thumb at his companion "This man will ask you what kind of sandwiches you want and they'll be brought to you. On the City of Albany. You're Theodolinda Bonner?"

"Yes."

"A policewoman will be here before long, in case a search of your persons is required."

"With consent," Steve Amsel said offensively.

"Certainly with consent. Nero Wolfe? Come along, you and Archie Goodwin."

Wolfe got up and headed for the door, saying, as he passed me, "Come, Archie." I was on his payroll, and he wasn't going to have other people giving me orders.

### III

There were three men in the hall, one in his own clothes, looking important, and two in uniform guarding an empty meat basket near the door of room thirty-eight, looking bored. Inside the room were three more—scientists, two with fingerprint outfits and one with a camera. They took time out to look as Groom, having told us to touch nothing, convoyed Wolfe around the table to the corpse. Except that its legs had been straightened and its necktie removed, it hadn't changed much. Wolfe frowned down at it.

Groom asked him, "Do you identify him?"

"No," Wolfe declared. "I don't know who he is. I do, however, recognize him as a man I saw one day last April when he called on me, gave his name as Otis Ross, and engaged my services. I learned later that he was not Otis Ross—at least not the Otis Ross he had claimed to be. Mr. Goodwin, who saw him not once but nine times, has already stated that he is that man."

"I know. Is that still your opinion, Goodwin?"

"Not an opinion." If Wolfe could correct his choice

of words so could I. "Conviction. He's that man—or was."

"Then we can—oh, by the way." He turned to the table, pointed to an object on it, and asked one of the scientists, "Are you through with this ashtray, Walsh?"

"All done, Captain. Got it."

"Then you can help a little, Goodwin, if you don't mind. Just an experiment. Take it and hold it the way you would to hit a man on the head with it. Just naturally, without thinking."

"Sure," I said, and reached to get it. Jiggling it, I would have said at least a pound and probably more. "There would be two ways, both good. Either take it by the rim, like this, that would be best if you had room and time to swing"—I swung to show him—"or, with a big mitt and long fingers like mine, just cup it, like this, and you could either swing or hook or jab." I performed a healthy jab, then transferred the tray to my left hand, got out my handkerchief with my right, and started wiping the brass with plenty of pressure.

"Not so good," Groom said. "Your slapstick may go over big down where you belong, but here in the City of Albany we don't appreciate it. It won't buy you a thing."

"What would?" I demanded. "What did you want me to do, refuse to touch it?" I finished the rubbing and put the tray back on the table.

"Come along," he said, and moved. We followed him out and down the hall nearly to the end, where he opened a door and stood aside for us to pass. This was a corner room with windows on two sides, and it sported a couple of rugs. Seated at a desk with a window behind him was Albert Hyatt, talking on the phone. A man with big ears and a scar on his cheek came toward us and asked Groom how he wanted the chairs. So Wolfe and I would face the window, naturally. By the time Hyatt finished on the phone we were disposed, with Wolfe and me side by side and the man with ears at a little table nearby, with a notebook in front of him and a pen ready.

Hyatt stood up and invited Groom to come and take the desk, and Groom said no thanks and kept his chair on this side of it, facing us. He focused on Wolfe. "Mr. Hyatt has let me read your statement. Your statement to the secretary of state regarding wiretapping. He has also told me what you said to him this morning—merely a repetition of parts of the statement. Do you now want to change it?"

"No, sir."

"Do you want to add anything to it?"

"That depends. If I am under suspicion of murder, or if Mr. Goodwin is, I wish to add something. Are we under suspicion?"

"Put it this way. You're not charged. You're being held for questioning, by police authority, to learn if you have any knowledge of the murder of a man with whom you admit you have been associated, and against whom you had a grievance. You did have a grievance?"

"I did indeed. I wish to make a further statement."

"Go ahead."

"I was summoned by the secretary of state to appear at this address in Albany at ten o'clock this morning. At six o'clock this morning I left my house in New York, in my car, with Mr. Goodwin driving. We stopped once en route, to eat something we had with us, and for coffee. We arrived at this address shortly before ten o'clock and entered the building, were directed to room forty-two on the third floor, went

straight there, speaking to no one, and I remained
there until I was taken to see Mr. Hyatt. Mr. Goodwin
was out of the room briefly, with Miss Sally Colt, to go
for coffee. I have not at any time seen or spoken to—
what am I to call that creature?"

"The murdered man?"

"Yes."

"Call him your client."

"I prefer not to, in this context. I've had other
clients. With regard to the man who called on me last
April and told me he was Otis Ross, and hired me to
do a job as described in my statement to the secretary
of state, I have never seen him or had any communication with him, or known anything of his where-
abouts, since April thirteenth, nineteen fifty-five. My
next knowledge of him was when, after leaving the
room with Mr. Hyatt this morning, Mr. Goodwin returned almost immediately to tell me that he was lying dead in a nearby room. My next sight of him was a
few minutes ago, when I was taken to that room and
saw him dead. I had not known that he was on the
premises. It is inane to pile up negatives. I have no
knowledge whatever of his death or of his movements
prior to his death. Beyond the facts given in my statement to the secretary of state, I have no knowledge of
any nature that might be of help in the investigation
of this murder."

Wolfe considered a moment. "There, Mr. Groom. I
don't see what good can come of questions, but certainly you can try."

"Yeah, I can always try." Groom looked at me, and
I thought it was my turn, but he went back to Wolfe.
"You say you entered this building this morning
shortly before ten o'clock. How much before?"

"Of my own knowledge, I don't know. I don't carry

a watch. But as we entered Mr. Goodwin remarked that it was five minutes to ten. He claims that he never allows his watch to be more than thirty seconds off."

"What time was it when you got to room forty-two?"

"I don't know. I can only estimate. I would say that it took us four minutes, to the elevator, up to the third floor, and down the hall to the room. That would make it one minute to ten."

"What if one or more of the others say that you arrived in the room about a quarter past ten?"

Wolfe eyed him. "Mr. Groom. That question is pointless and you know it. As a menace it is puerile. As a mere hypothesis it is flippant. And if one of them does say that you know how many issues it will raise, including his candor. Or more than one—even all of them. If you want your question answered as you put it, either his timepiece was wrong or his memory is at fault or he lies."

"Yeah." Apparently Groom was hard to rile. He shifted to me. "Naturally you corroborate everything Wolfe has said. Do you?"

"Naturally," I told him.

"Yes or no. Do you?"

"Yes."

"Including the time of your arrival at this building?"

"Yes. Nine-fifty-five."

He got up and stepped to me. "Let's see your watch."

I twisted my arm around and pushed the shirt cuff back, and he took a look, then looked at his own, then back at mine. He told the man at the table, "Put it that I found Goodwin's watch twenty seconds slow," and returned to his chair.

"You may wonder," he said, "why I didn't take you two separately. Because it would have been a waste of time. From what I know of your reputations and records and how you work, I figured that if you had fixed up a story the chance of my getting you to cross was so slim that it wasn't worth the trouble. Also Mr. Hyatt wanted to go to lunch, and I wanted him with us, and you might as well know why." He turned. "Will you tell them what you told me, Mr. Hyatt?"

Hyatt's strand of hair was back in place again. He was leaning forward with his elbows on the desk. "You mean about this morning?" he asked Groom.

"Yes. Just that."

"Well, I got here early, a little before nine o'clock. One of my staff, Tom Frazer, was already here. We were here at this desk together, going over papers, getting ready for those who were to appear today, when the girl phoned me that a man wanted to see me about something that he said was urgent and confidential, he wouldn't say what. He gave the name of Donahue, which meant nothing to me. I didn't want him interrupting in here, so I went out front to get rid of him and found him on a bench in the hall. He wouldn't talk in the hall, so I took him to the nearest empty room, room thirty-eight. He was a middle-aged man, about my height, brown hair and eyes—"

"They've seen him," Groom put in.

"Oh." Hyatt was fussed. "So they have. He said his name was William A. Donahue and he wanted to make a deal. He said he knew who was due to appear before me today, and that Nero Wolfe was one of them, and that he had got cold feet and wanted to get from under. His terms. Must I give the whole conversation, Captain? We talked for some twenty minutes."

"The substance will do. The main points."

"There was only one main point, actually. He floundered around a good deal, but this was the gist of it. In connection with a venture he was engaged in, he didn't say what, he had procured some wiretapping operations, one of them through Nero Wolfe, for which he had paid Wolfe two thousand dollars. When the scandal started—he called it the big stink—and Broady was arrested and indicted, he had decided New York was too hot for him and had left the state. When he learned recently that this inquiry was to be held by the secretary of state, and that all private detectives were to be questioned, he had become alarmed, particularly on account of Nero Wolfe. Wolfe had abruptly called off the tap he had handled for him, and they had had a row, and Wolfe had it in for him. He knew how tricky Wolfe was, and now that he had been summoned—am I confusing you with my pronouns?"

He was looking at Wolfe, so Wolfe replied. "Not at all. Go on."

"—And now that Wolfe had been summoned, he knew he would try to wriggle out of it somehow or other, and that he—Donahue—would get hooked for something worse than procurement of illegal wiretapping. So he wanted to make a deal with me. If I would use my influence with the district attorney to go easy with him on the wiretapping charges, he would give me a full account of the operation, under oath, and would testify in court as required. I asked him if Wolfe had known the tap was illegal, and he said yes. I asked him if Donahue was his real name, and if he had given that name to Wolfe, and he said yes. I asked to get Wolfe and Donahue face to face and see what happened, and I went to the hearing room and sent for Wolfe and Goodwin." Hyatt looked at his watch. "I'm late for a lunch appointment."

"Yeah, I know." Groom looked at Wolfe. "You want to ask Mr. Hyatt anything?"

Wolfe had his legs crossed, as usual when he was on a chair too small for him and without arms. He uncrossed them and put his palms on his knees. "Just a question or two. You will remember, Mr. Hyatt, that you told me that you personally credited my story. Why did you tell me that?"

"Because I meant it."

"You had already talked with this Donahue."

"Yes, but I hadn't believed him. I know something of your record and standing, and I knew nothing whatever of his. On the simple issue of veracity I preferred you, at least tentatively."

"Do you still credit my story?"

"Well . . ." Hyatt looked at Groom and back at Wolfe. "Under the present circumstances I'm afraid my personal opinion is neither relevant nor cogent."

"I suppose not. One other thing. This Donahue said he had procured some wiretapping operations. Plural. Did he mention any names other than mine?"

"Yes, he mentioned others, but he concentrated on you throughout the conversation."

"What other names did he mention?"

"Just a minute," Groom cut in. "I don't think that's called for. We won't keep you any longer, Mr. Hyatt."

"I want to know," Wolfe insisted, "if that man mentioned the names of any of the others summoned here today."

He had to keep on wanting. Hyatt looked at Groom, Groom shook his head, and Hyatt got up and

him for further information about himself, and h
wouldn't give me any until and unless I agreed to his
proposal—except one item, that in New York he had
lived at the Hotel Marbury. I told him I couldn't make
such a deal offhand, I'd have to think it over a little,
and told him to wait there in the room and left him
there, and came back to this room and—"

"What time was it then?" Groom asked.

"It was half past nine, a minute or two after. I
don't keep my watch as close to the dot as Goodwin
does, but it's fairly accurate." He looked at his wrist.
"I've got one-forty-two."

"You're three minutes fast."

"Then it was about exactly nine-thirty when I returned to this room." He went back to Wolfe. "I
looked, of course, to see how much time I had. The
hearing was supposed to begin at ten. I thought it was
important enough to consult the secretary of state
about it, so I called his office, but was told that he was
in New York for a conference and his secretary didn't
know where I could reach him at that hour. I phoned
the office of the district attorney of New York County
and got Assistant DA Lambert, a friend of mine, and
told him I wanted an emergency police report on a
William A. Donahue who had lived last spring at the
Hotel Marbury, as quickly as possible. At a quarter
past ten I had had no word, and I tried to get the
executive deputy secretary of state on the wire, but
he wasn't in his office. I told Tom Frazer all about it,
and—"

Groom stopped him. "I think that'll do. You didn't
go back to room thirty-eight to see Donahue."

"No. I had told him it would take an hour or more,
possibly two. When no report had come from New
York at eleven o'clock—none has come yet—I decided

went. Wolfe crossed his legs again, and also his arms, but the props weren't right. He never was as impressive when he was on a chair that allowed portions of his fundament to lap over at the edges of the seat. When the door had closed behind the special deputy of the secretary of state, Groom spoke. "I wanted you to hear that direct from Mr. Hyatt. It's neater that way. Do you want to change your statement now? Or add to it? Of course Donahue's dead, but we've got his track and we know where to dig. You know how that is."

"Yes, I know." Wolfe grunted "I like to talk, Mr. Groom, but not to no purpose. As for changing my statement, I might improve its diction or its punctuation, but materially, no. As for adding to it, I might make a few footnotes, as for instance that that man lied when he told Mr. Hyatt that he had given me his name as Donahue, and that I knew that the tap was illegal, but they are already implicit in the statement. I do have a request to make. I now have his name, at least the name he gave Mr. Hyatt, and the name of the hotel where he lived at the time he called on me. I can be of no use to you here. I have absolutely nothing for you; and if I am permitted to return to New York at once I shall devote all my talents and resources to the exposure of his background, his activities, his connections with—"

He stopped because Groom had turned his head. Groom had turned his head because the door had opened and a man was approaching, a colleague in uniform. The cop came to him, said, "For you, Captain," and handed him a folded paper. Groom unfolded the paper, gave it a look, taking his time, told the cop to stick around, glanced at the paper again, and lifted his eyes to Wolfe and me.

"This is a warrant," he said, "for your arrest as material witnesses in a murder case. I hereby serve it. Do you want to see it?"

I turned my head to Wolfe. I can testify that through a full ten-second silence his lids didn't blink once. Then he spoke, but all he said was, "No."

"I do," I said, and put out a hand, and Groom handed it over. It looked kosher, and even had our names spelled right. The signature of the judge looked like Bymnyomr. "I guess it's real," I told Wolfe.

He was regarding Groom. "I hardly know," he said icily, "the word to use. High-handed? Bumptious? Headstrong?"

"You're not in New York now, Wolfe." Groom was trying not to show how much he liked himself. "This is the City of Albany. I'll ask you once more, do you want to change your statement or add to it?"

"You actually mean to serve this thing?"

"I *have* served it. You're under arrest."

Wolfe turned to me. "What's Mr. Parker's number?"

"Eastwood six two-six-oh-five."

He arose, circled around the desk to the chair Hyatt had vacated, sat, and took the phone from the cradle. Groom got to his feet, took a step, stopped, stood, and stuck his hands in his pockets. Wolfe took the phone. "A New York City call, please. Eastwood six two-six-oh-five."

Four hours later, at six o'clock, we were still in the coop. Of course I had been behind bars before, but never together with Wolfe. For him it was a first, since I had known him.

Actually we weren't behind bars, or at least none were visible. It was a detention room at police headquarters, and wasn't bad at all, except that it smelled like a hospital in the middle of the Jersey marshes and the chairs were greasy. There was even a private john in a closet in a corner. A cop was there with us, presumably to see that we didn't cheat the chair by making a suicide pact and carrying it out. When I told him an evening paper would be worth a buck to us he opened the door and yelled down the hall to someone, sticking to his post. Taking no chances.

Soon after our incarceration we had been told we could send out for grub, and I had ordered two corned-beef sandwiches on white toast and a quart of milk. Wolfe, who had swallowed nothing but coffee since ten o'clock, declined the offer. Whether he was staging a hunger strike or was just too mad to eat, I couldn't say. When my corned beef on white toast arrived it turned out to be ham on rye, and the ham was only so-so, but the milk was okay.

Not only was Wolfe not eating in captivity, also he wasn't talking. Keeping his hat on, he sat on his overcoat spread on an old wooden bench against the wall, mostly leaning back with his eyes closed and his fingers interlaced at the summit of his central mound. Looking at him, and I had seen a lot of him, I would say that instead of calming down he kept getting madder. His only real try at communication, after a couple of hours had passed, was when he opened his eyes and told me he wanted my true opinion about something. I said he could have my true opinion about everything, and apparently we'd have plenty of time for it.

He grunted. "I foresee that in the future, if you and I continue to be associated, as we probably shall, this episode will be frequently mentioned, in one context or another. Do you agree?"

"I do. Provided it's not our last episode. You're assuming we'll have a future."

"Pfui. We'll see to that. Answer this. If you had not been seduced by your itch to have a hand in a wiretapping operation and to observe the procedure and technique, do you think I would have undertaken that job for that man? I'm merely asking for your opinion."

"Well, you won't get it." I stood looking down at him. "If I say no, the future mentions would be too one-sided. If I say yes, it would pile one more provocation on the load you're already carrying, and it might be too much for you. You can't think us out of this if you're boiling too high to think. So I'll tell you what I'll do: I'll split it."

"Split what?"

"The blame. Fifty-fifty. We both ought to be larruped. But not fried."

"We'll leave it to the future," he growled, and shut his eyes on me.

At six o'clock I was deep in the second section of the evening paper, reading how to repair nylon brassieres that had got torn somehow, having covered other matters, when the door was flung open. Our guard whirled on his heels, ready to repel an attempt at armed rescue, but it was only a cop conducting a

visitor. The visitor, a red-faced guy in a brown cash-
mere overcoat, stopped for a glance around and then
came on and put out a hand.

"Mr. Wolfe? I'm Stanley Rogers. I'm terribly
sorry. I suppose you thought I'd fallen in a hole and
pulled the hole in, but Nat Parker didn't get me until
nearly three o'clock, and the judge was in the middle
of a case and I had to pull some strings. We're not
being very hospitable up here, are we? This is Mr.
Goodwin? It's a pleasure." He offered a hand, and I
took it. "I asked the judge to make the bail figure five
thousand, but he wouldn't settle for less than twenty.
Twenty thousand each. Anyhow, you're free men, as I
have no doubt you deserve to be, only you can't leave
the jurisdiction without permission of the court. I've
reserved a room for you at the Latham Hotel, but of
course it can be canceled if you want to make other
arrangements."

He had some papers for us to sign. He said that
Parker, phoning from New York, had told him to do
everything possible for us, and he would cancel a dinner appointment if we wanted him, but Wolfe said
that at the moment all he wanted was to get out of
there and find something to eat. One offer we took.
He had his car out front, and after telling the guard
good-by, no tip, and going to an office to check out and
claim some personal articles we had been relieved of,
he led us out to it and drove us to the garage where
we had left the sedan. With Wolfe in back again, I
drove to the hotel, got the bags from the trunk, and
turned the car over to a lackey.

About the bags, I could have told Wolfe I had told
him so, but decided he was in no shape for it. The
evening before, pigheaded as usual, he had refused to
admit the possibility of spending a night away from

home and insisted that we would need no luggage, but I had packed his bag myself, with some help from Fritz, on the theory that man proposes but some other specimen may dispose. Now, as the bellboy followed us into room 902 and put the bags on the rack, it was a fine opportunity for a casual cutting remark, but I thought it advisable to save it.

His overcoat hung in the closet, along with mine, Wolfe removed his coat, vest, tie, and shirt, and went to the bathroom and washed his hands and face. Emerging, he put on his dressing gown, a yellow wool number with fine black stripes, got his slippers, sat on a chair to take off his shoes, and told me to phone room service to send up a menu. I reminded him that Rogers had told us the Latham grub was only fair and that the best restaurant in town was only two blocks away.

"I'm not interested," he declared. "I have no appetite, and will have no palate. I eat because I must. You know quite well I can't work on an empty stomach."

So he was going to work.

I don't remember a gloomier meal. The food was perfectly edible—oysters, consommé, roast beef, creamed potatoes, broccoli, salad, apple pie with cheese, coffee—and we cleaned it up, but the atmosphere had no sparkle. Though Wolfe never talks business at the table, he likes to talk while eating, about anything and everything but business, and nearly always does. That time he didn't utter a single word from beginning to end, and I made no effort to start him. Finishing his second cup of coffee, he pushed his chair back and muttered at me, "What time is it?"

I looked. "Twenty after eight."

"Well." He pulled air in through his mouth all the

way down to the roast beef, and let it out through his nose. "I don't know if you realize the pickle I'm in."

"The pickle is split too. Fifty-fifty."

"Only to a point. The jeopardy, yes, but I have a special difficulty. We're going to be held here until this case is solved. I can hurry our release only by solving it, but I don't want to. Certainly people cannot be permitted to murder with impunity, but I would prefer to have no hand in exposing the man who killed that abominable creature. What am I to do?"

I waved a hand. "That's easy. Sit it out. This room isn't so bad. You can go to sessions of the state legislature when it meets, and get books from the library, and I can teach Sally Colt things if she's hung up here too. If it drags on into months, as it probably will if that Groom is the best they've got, we can rent a little apartment and send for Fritz—"

"Shut up."

"Yes, sir. Or perhaps Sally and I could solve it without you. I don't feel as grateful to the bird who did it as you seem to. If—"

"Bosh. I am not grateful. I wanted to see him again alive. Very well. As between the intolerable and the merely distasteful, I must choose the latter. I presume the others are also being held in the jurisdiction."

"If you mean our confreres, sure they are. Maybe not arrested like us, but held, certainly. Groom's not sold on us enough to let them go, and anyway Hyatt wants them for his hearing."

He nodded. "I have to see them. Some of them may be in this hotel. Find them and bring them here."

"Now?"

"Yes."

"Have you any suggestions?"

"No. My mind's not in order. I'll try to get it arranged by the time you get them."

That had happened before, many times. He knew
that my only alternatives were either to protest that
he was biting off more than I could chew, or to take it
as a compliment that if he wanted a miracle passed all
he had to do was snap his fingers at me; and also he
knew which I would pick.

"Okay," I told him. "Then will you please phone
room service to come and get the dishes? And you
might as well phone Fritz so he won't start worrying.
I've got some thinking to do."

I went to a window, parted the curtains, put the
blind up, and stood looking down at the street by
night. It wasn't the first time I had been given the
chore of setting up a party, but it had never been with
a gang of private dicks, and they would need something special. Brilliant ideas started coming. Tell them
Wolfe thought they would be interested to hear what
Hyatt had asked him at the hearing. Tell them Wolfe
had an idea for getting all of us released from the
jurisdiction and wanted to consult with them. Tell
them Wolfe had certain information about the murdered man which he had not given to the police and
wanted to discuss it. Tell them that Wolfe thought it
was important to fix the time of arrival of each of us at
room 42 and wanted us to get together on it. And so
on, up to a dozen or so. I rattled them around in my
skull. The idea was to get one that would work with
all of them.

Suddenly I remembered that Wolfe had once told
me that the best way to choose among an assortment
of ideas was to take the simplest. I pulled the blind
down and turned. He had just finished talking to Fritz
and was lowering himself into the chair with arms,

which was almost wide enough. I asked him, "You want them together, don't you?"

He said yes.

"How soon?"

"Oh . . . twenty minutes. Half an hour."

I went and sat on the edge of one of the beds, lifted the phone, and told the girl I understood Mr. Harland Ide was registered and would she please ring his room. In two moments his bass, a little hoarse, told me hello.

"Mr. Harland Ide?"

"Speaking."

"This is Archie Goodwin. I'm calling for Mr. Wolfe. We're in room nine-oh-two. He would like very much to consult you about something, not on the phone. Right now he's resting. If you'll do him the favor of dropping in at room nine-oh-two, say in half an hour, he'll appreciate it very much. Say nine o'clock. We hope you will."

A brief silence. "Could you give me an idea?"

"Better not, on the phone."

A slightly longer silence. "All right, I'll be there."

The simplest is the best. Of course their being private detectives was a big advantage. Tell any private detective you want to discuss something that is too hot for the phone, and he'll swim a river to get to you.

They weren't all quite as simple as Ide. Steve Amsel wasn't registered at the Latham, but I got him at another hotel and sold him on the trip. Jay Kerr was at the Latham, but his line was busy the first two tries and I got him last. Dol Bonner and Sally Colt were on our floor, room 917, and I wished I had gone down the hall and dined with them instead of putting up with a dummy. At first Dol Bonner didn't care for the idea, but when I told her the others were coming she said we could expect her. Having got Kerr on the third try, I hung up and turned to Wolfe. "All set. Want anyone else? Groom? Hyatt? The secretary of state?"

"What time is it?"

"Nine minutes to nine."

"Confound it, I must dress." He arose and started peeling the dressing gown. He wasn't going to receive females in negligee, especially in a hotel room.


# V


It was a good-sized room and wasn't too crowded with seven people, or, counting Wolfe as two, eight. I had phoned down a rush order for four more chairs, so no one had to perch on a bed. Dol Bonner and Sally, still sticking close, were over by the wall. Steve Amsel, next to them, had turned his chair around and folded his arms on top of its back, with his chin resting on his wrist. He was still very neat, and his black eyes were still quick. Harland Ide looked tired, but still dignified enough for a banker. Jay Kerr, the half-bald roly-poly, was the last one to show. He brought along two clues that were spotted immediately by my highly trained powers of observation: a flushed face and a breath.

"Well well!" he exclaimed at sight of us. "A party, huh? You didn't tell me, Archie. Well well!"

"Siddown and listen," Amsel commanded him. "We waited for you. Wolfe wants to sing a song."

"That I'd like to hear," Kerr said cordially, and sat.

Wolfe's eyes went around. "I think the best way to begin," he said, "is to read you the statement I submitted to the secretary of state." He took a document from his pocket and unfolded it. "It's rather long, but I want you to know my position. If you'll permit me."

"Sure," Kerr told him. "Shoot."

He started reading. It took a full ten minutes, but he held his audience. I must admit I felt for him. What he would have liked to do with that affair was scrap it and try to forget it, but, having already been compelled to record it in a sworn statement and to recite it to Hyatt, he now had to spill it again to a collection of his fellow members of a professional association. It must have been about the bitterest pill he ever had to take, but he got it down. When he got to the end he refolded it and handed it to me.

He rested his elbows on the chair arms and matched his fingertips. "So this morning I couldn't tell you the name of the murdered man. I spoke then of my ignominy, and I won't dwell on it. Do any of you want anything in the statement clarified? Any questions?"

Apparently nobody had any. Wolfe resumed, "Mr. Goodwin told you on the phone that I wanted to consult you about something. It is this. We are all involved in an investigation of a murder and are under restraint. Mr. Goodwin and I have been arrested as material witnesses and released on bail. I don't know if any of you have been arrested, but certainly your movements have been restricted. I think it will be to our common advantage to pool our information, discuss it, and decide what can be done with it. We are all trained and experienced investigators."

Amsel started to speak, but Wolfe raised a hand. "If you please. Before you comment, let me say that neither Mr. Goodwin nor I had anything to do with that man's death, nor have we any knowledge of it. Possibly that is true of all of you. If so, the worth of

my suggestion is manifest; we would be nincompoops
not to share our information and join our wits. If not,
if one of you killed him or had a hand in it, he certainly
won't tell us so, and probably he will be reluctant to
give us any information at all; but obviously it would
be to the interest of the rest of us to merge our knowledge and our resources. Don't you agree?"

For the first time they exchanged glances. Jay
Kerr said, "Pretty neat. Well well! Last one in is a
monkey."

"You put it good," Amsel declared. "If I don't play
I'm it."

"I have a question." It was Harland Ide. "Why
were you and Goodwin arrested and put under bail?"

"Because," Wolfe told him, "that man—I presume
you all know by now that his name was Donahue—
because he told Mr. Hyatt a story this morning which
conflicted with my statement. He said that he had
given me his name as Donahue and that I knew the
tap was illegal."

"Ouch," Kerr said. "No wonder you want us to
open up."

"I have opened up, Mr. Kerr. I'll answer any questions you care to ask. And I assure you I'm not im-
pelled by any fear of ultimate disaster, either for Mr.
Goodwin or for myself. I merely want to go home."

Dol Bonner spoke up. "It seems to me," she said,
"that the only question is whether it will do any good
or not. It can't do any harm. We have already given
the police all the information we have, at least I have
and Miss Colt has, and tomorrow they'll be at us
again." She directed the caramel-colored eyes at
Wolfe. "What good will it do?"

He frowned at her. Sometimes he honestly tries to
speak to a woman without frowning at her, but he

seldom makes it. "Possibly none, madam. But among us we pretend to a considerable batch of gumption, and we may even have it. If so, we might as well use it, since our only alternative is to sit and brood, hoping that Mr. Groom has either brains or luck. Have you people compared notes at all?"

He got three noes and two headshakes.

"Then it's about time. You don't even know whether one or more of you can safely be eliminated. Assuming that one of us killed him, do you know what the time limits are? . . . You don't. Evidently you haven't had the privilege, as I have, of hearing Mr. Hyatt's story. The murder was committed between nine-thirty, when Mr. Hyatt left Donahue alone in the room, and ten o'clock, when Mr. Goodwin and I arrived. Assuming that one of us killed him—an assumption we must accept unless we find an excuse for discarding it. Therefore if one or more of you can establish that you arrived in room forty-two before nine-thirty, and stayed there, you're out of it. Can you?"

"Not me," Dol Bonner said. "Miss Colt and I were there first, at twenty minutes to ten. About five minutes later Mr. Ide came, and in another four or five minutes Mr. Amsel. Next was Mr. Kerr, and you and Mr. Goodwin came last, just before ten o'clock. I resented it when you were called in because we got there first and I thought we should be called first."

"Then we're still intact. When I said the limits are nine-thirty and ten o'clock I ignored the possibility that when Mr. Goodwin and Miss Colt went for coffee one of them, or both, stopped in at room thirty-eight and killed him. Does anyone want to explore it?"

Sally Colt started to titter. It was a flaw in her, but I made allowances because it could have been the first time she had been at close quarters with a murder, and naturally she was strung tight. I came to the rescue. "Cross it off. I didn't, she didn't, and we didn't."

"Miss Colt?"

"Don't be silly!" Her voice was louder than necessary, and she lowered it. "No. Mr. Goodwin is correct."

"Good. He often is." Wolfe shifted in his chair. His rump had taken a lot of punishment since six o'clock that morning. "Presumably the police theory is that one of us, going along the hall on arrival, caught sight of Donahue, who could have opened the door of the room to look out, and proceeded to finish him. Under that theory we're at the crux. There couldn't have been time for a prolonged conversation unless the murderer entered the building much earlier than he arrived at room forty-two, and in that case the police will probably get him without any help from us. The point is that in all probability the mere sight of Donahue on those premises was enough to make the murderer resolve on his death forthwith. Do any of you qualify? I have reported to you fully and candidly on my association with that man. Did any of you have dealings with him?"

"I did," Dol Bonner said.

"Yes, Miss Bonner? Will you elaborate?"

"Certainly. I've told the police, so why not you?" There was an edge of scorn on her voice, either for Wolfe or for the others, no telling. "First, though, I left something out, not deliberately. When Miss Colt and I got to the third floor of that building I went to the women's room and she went on to room forty-two. It was twenty minutes to ten when I joined her there. The police know that too, of course. Also I heard a police detective telling a man—I think it was the district attorney—that all of us had recognized the body."

"Indeed." Wolfe's frown was about gone. "All of you?"

"That's what he said." Her eyes went to Ide, to Amsel, to Kerr, and back to Wolfe. "About my dealings with him, they were almost identical with yours. He came to my office last April and gave his name as Alan Samuels, and wanted me to arrange for a wiretap on the telephone at his home—a house in the Bronx—with exactly the same arrangement he made with you. I didn't have an Archie Goodwin to nudge me on, but I thought it wouldn't hurt any for me to learn something about wiretapping if I could do it legitimately, and I agreed to handle it if he would establish his identity. He showed me some papers—a driver's license and some letters—but I told him that wasn't enough."

She stopped to swallow. Evidently she wasn't any prouder of her performance than Wolfe was of his. "He said he had an account in a bank around the corner—my office is at Fiftieth and Madison—and asked me to go there with him. I had an appointment and couldn't leave the office, so I asked Miss Colt to go." She turned. "Sally, that's your part."

Sally wasn't looking very gay. "You want me to tell it?"

Dol Bonner said yes, and Sally gave Wolfe her eyes. From my angle, in the electric light, the blue in them didn't show; they looked almost as black as Amsel's. "Miss Bonner told me what was required," she said, "and I went with him around the corner to the Madison Avenue branch of the Continental Trust Company. He took me through the gate in the railing to where there were four men at desks, and went to one of the desks. There was a little stand on the desk with a name on it, Frederick Poggett. The client called the man at the desk Mr. Poggett, and shook hands with him, and told him that in connection with a business transaction he needed to establish his identity, and would Mr. Poggett please identify him. Mr. Poggett said of course, and turned to me and said, 'This gentleman is Mr. Samuels, a customer of our bank.' I said, 'Alan Samuels?' and he said yes, and then told the client that if it was a matter of credit he would be glad to verify his balance. The client said that wouldn't be necessary, and we left. We went back to the office and I reported to Miss Bonner."

She stopped and looked at Dol Bonner, who nodded and took the ball. "In my case, Mr. Wolfe, it wasn't his secretary he suspected, it was his brother who was living in his house, but that's just a detail. He paid me in cash, a thousand dollars, and I found out how to arrange for the tap and did so. He was to come to the office at five o'clock every day for the report. The morning after he had got the fifth report he phoned to say that he didn't need the tap any longer and asked if he owed me anything. I told him yes, another five hundred dollars, and in an hour or so he came in and paid it."

She made a little gesture. "I never did suspect him. I still say there was no reason to. But when all the publicity about wiretapping started, and then when we were told to report under oath any and all connections we had had with wiretapping, I went to the bank and spoke with Mr. Poggett, taking Miss Colt with me. He remembered the incident, of course. After going to look at the records, he told me that Alan Samuels had opened a checking account at the bank on February eighteenth, giving a business address on Lexington Avenue. He, Poggett, had attended to it. He wouldn't tell me either the amount or the references Samuels had given, but he did tell me that the balance had been withdrawn, closing the account, on April twentieth, which was the day after Samuels had canceled the tap, and I did get the Lexington Avenue address out of him. Of course I suspected I had been taken in, and I—do you want me to go on? My efforts to trace him?"

"Not unless you found him. Did you?"

"No. I never did. The next time I saw him was in that room today. Dead."

"You didn't see him alive first?"

"I did not."

"Wouldn't it have been a simple matter to check on your suspicion—either confirm it or allay it?"

"Oh." She was taken aback. "I left that out. Of course. I went myself to the address in the Bronx. A man named Alan Samuels lived there, but he wasn't the same man."

"Did you tell him of your—uh, inadvertent invasion of his privacy?"

"No. I admit I should have, but I didn't. I was sick about it, and I was sick of it."

"Did you inform yourself about him—his occupation, his standing, his interests?"

"No. What good would that do?"

"What is his address?"

"I don't . . ." She hesitated. "Is that important?"

Wolfe was frowning at her again. "Come, Miss Bonner. When a Bronx phone book will probably supply it?"

She flushed a little. "It merely seems to me that

it's immaterial. Twenty-nine seventy Borchard Avenue, the Bronx."

Wolfe turned. "Archie. Get Mr. Cohen. Give him that name and address and tell him we would like to have such information as is readily available. Within an hour if possible."

I got up and went to the phone. The number of the *Gazette* was one I didn't have to consult my notebook for. I told them to go right ahead, that I was used to phoning under difficulties, but they politely kept silence. At that evening hour I had New York in twenty seconds, got Lon, and made the request, but it took two minutes to get rid of him. He wanted an exclusive on how we had got arrested and on the kind of knot I had used on Donahue's necktie, and I had to get rude and hang up on him. As I returned to my chair Wolfe invited the audience, "Do any of you want to ask Miss Bonner any questions?"

Apparently they didn't.

"I think," he said, "that we can best show our appreciation of Miss Bonner's candor by reciprocating it. Mr. Ide? Mr. Amsel? Mr. Kerr?"

Ide sat and pinched the skin over his Adam's apple. Amsel, his arms still folded on the back of his chair, kept his eyes at Wolfe. Jay Kerr made a noise, but it was only a minor belch.

"I can understand," Wolfe said, "that by your vocation and training you have developed a high regard for discretion, but I hope you haven't made a fetish of it. According to Miss Bonner, all of you recognized the dead man. In that case, not only had you met him, but also you had met him under circumstances that made you think it hazardous, or at least imprudent, to pretend to no knowledge of him. As Miss Bonner said, what you have told the police can surely be told here, unless you have reason to fear—"

"What the hell," Jay Kerr blurted. "Sure, I knew the bastard."

"There's ladies here," Amsel reproached him.

"They're not ladies, they're fellow members. Why, wasn't he a bastard? Look how he played Wolfe and Dol Bonner, two professionals of the highest standards. A skunk. I'll be glad to ante all I know about him, but I want a drink first."

"I beg your pardon," Wolfe apologized, and he meant it. "Away from home I'm not myself, and I even neglect the amenities. Archie? If you please?"


# VI

For Dol Bonner it was brandy and coffee, for Sally rum and coke, another flaw, for Ide tea with lemon, for Amsel double bourbon with water, for Kerr double scotch on the rocks, for Wolfe two bottles of beer, and for me double milk. I like a drink occasionally, but not when I'm out on bail. Then I need all my faculties.

Kerr had said he wanted a drink first, so while we waited for the supplies to come up Wolfe went back to some details with Dol Bonner, such as the date Donahue had first called on her, but that was just to pass the time. Or maybe not. I was glad Fritz wasn't there. He suspects every woman who ever crosses the threshold of wanting to take over his kitchen, not to mention the rest of the house. He would have been squirming. Dol Bonner's caramel-colored eyes and long dark lashes were by no means her only physical attractions, and she was the right age, she had shown some sense and had done a pretty good job of reporting, and she was a companion in misery, having also been made a monkey of by Donahue. Of course if Wolfe hung a murder on her she would no longer be a danger, but I noticed that he had stopped frowning at her. Oh well, I thought, if she hooks him and Sally hooks me we can all solve cases together and dominate the field.

After the drinks had come and been distributed, and Wolfe had taken a couple of healthy gulps of beer, he focused on Jay Kerr. "Yes, sir? You were going to tell us."

Kerr was sipping his scotch. "He played me too. Good. Only not the same pattern exactly. What was eating him was his wife. He wanted his home tapped, an apartment in Brooklyn. He wanted full reports on all voices, male and female, because he thought there might be a male around when he was away that shouldn't be there. I can tell you and Miss Bonner too, you got gypped. He gave me two thousand at the go and another pair later."

"Thank you. I'll demand more next time. When was this?"

"It was early April when he contacted me. After two weeks, sixteen days if I remember right, he called the tap off and settled up."

"What was his name? The name he gave."

Kerr took a sip, swallowed, and made a face. "This whiskey don't taste right, but that's not the whiskey's fault. I had cabbage for dinner. About his name, well, the name he gave was Leggett. Arthur M. Leggett."

"That sounds familiar. L-e-g-g-e-double-t?"

"That's right."

"I've seen it. Archie?"

"Yeah," I agreed. "He's the head of something."

"He's the president," Dol Bonner said, "of the Metropolitan Citizens League."

That woman was getting on my nerves. Now she was giving him information he had asked me for and hadn't got, and they weren't even engaged yet. Wolfe thanked her courteously. Courtesy is okay, but I hoped he wasn't making a fetish of it. He asked Kerr, "How did he establish his identity?"

"He didn't."

Kerr took another sip and made another face, and Wolfe turned to me and said sharply, "Taste that whiskey."

I had had the same idea myself. It was beginning to look as if we might have a murderer with us, and not only that, it hadn't been long since a guy named Assa, right in our office, had swallowed a drink that had been served to him by me and had dropped dead. Cyanide. Wolfe didn't want a rerun of that one, and neither did I. I went and asked Kerr to let me taste it, and he said what the hell but handed it over. I took in a dribble, distributed it with my tongue, let it trickle down, repeated the performance with a thimbleful, and handed it back to him.

"Okay," I told Wolfe. "It must be the cabbage."

He grunted. "You say he didn't establish his identity, Mr. Kerr? Why not?"

"Why should he?" Kerr demanded. "Do you know how many husbands in the metropolitan area get suspicious about their wives every week on an average? Hundreds. Thousands! Some of them come to me for help. A man comes and wants to pay me for expert service. Why should I doubt if he knows who he is? If I tried to check on all of them I'd spend all my time on it."

"You must have heard that name, Arthur M. Leggett. A man of your widespread—uh, activities."

Kerr jerked his chin up. "Look, are you a cop? Or one of us?"

"I'm one of us."

"Then be yourself. Let the cops tell me what names I must have heard. Don't worry, they have and they will. And I reported the tap in my statement to the secretary of state, because it was ethical and because I knew I had to. I knew they had two of the technicians singing, and I would have been sunk if they connected me with a job I hadn't reported."

Wolfe nodded. "We have no desire to harass you, Mr. Kerr. We only ask that you contribute your share to our pool of information. You had no suspicion that your client was not Arthur M. Leggett?"

"No."

"And never have had?"

"No."

"Then when you were taken to view the corpse today you must have identified it as Arthur M. Leggett."

"I did."

"I see." Wolfe considered a moment. "Why not? And naturally, when you learned that wasn't his name you were shocked and indignant, and now you have severe epithets for him. You're not alone in that. So have I; so has Miss Bonner; and so, doubtless, have Mr. Ide and Mr. Amsel." He emptied his beer glass, refilled it, kept his eye on it long enough to see that the rising foam didn't break at the edge, then looked up. "Have you, Mr. Ide?"

Ide put his cup and saucer down on my suitcase, there on the rack, which I had invited him to use for a table. He cleared his throat. "I want to say, Mr. Wolfe, that I feel better than I did when I entered this room."

"Good. Since it's my room, and Mr. Goodwin's, I am gratified."

"Yes, sir. The fact is, my experience with that man was very similar to yours and Miss Bonner's, and I have deeply regretted it. He imposed on me as he did on you, and in the same pattern. If I gave you all the details it would be mostly a repetition of what you and Miss Bonner have said."

"Nevertheless, we'd like to hear them."

"I see no point in it."

Ide's voice had sharpened a little, but Wolfe stayed affable. "One or more of the details might be suggestive. Or at least corroborative. When did it happen?"

"In April."

"How much did he pay you?"

"Two thousand dollars."

"Did he give his name as Donahue?"

"No. Another name. As I said, the pattern was very similar to the one he used with you."

"How did he establish his identity?"

"I prefer not to say. I mishandled it badly. I omitted that detail from my statement to the secretary of state. I suppose Mr. Hyatt will insist on it at the hearing, but I don't think the whole thing will be published, and I'm not going to publish it by telling it here. I was going to say, the reason I feel better is that now I have the consolation of knowing that I'm not the only one he made a fool of."

"You have indeed. We have all qualified for dunce's caps." Wolfe drank some beer and passed his tongue over his lips. "How did it end? Did you get onto him, or did he call it off as he did with Miss Bonner and Mr. Kerr?"

"I prefer not to say." From the expression on Ide's bony face, with its long hawk's nose, he would prefer to switch to some harmless topic like the weather. "I'll say this much, the tap was discontinued after ten days, and that ended my association with him. Like you and Miss Bonner and Mr. Kerr, I never saw him again until today, and then he was a corpse."

"And you identified the corpse?"

"Yes. There was no other . . . it would have been folly not to."

"You identified it with the name he gave you when he hired you?"

"Of course."

"What was that name?"

Ide shook his head. "It was the name of a respectable and law-abiding citizen. I saw him and told him about it, and he was good enough to accept my apology. He is a very fine man. I hope his name won't have to be dragged into a murder case, and it won't be by me."

"But you have given it to the police, of course."

"No, not yet. I admit I may be compelled to. I can't let my career end by having my license taken away."

Wolfe's eyes went around. "I suggest that we leave the question open whether Mr. Ide has contributed his share, at least until we have heard from Mr. Amsel." They settled on Steve Amsel. "Well, sir?"

"If I don't play I'm it," Amsel said. "Huh?"

"It's not quite as simple as that," Wolfe told him. "But you've heard us, and it's your turn."

"Last one in is a monkey," Kerr declared.

"Nuts. Have I been last?" There was half a finger left of his double bourbon and water, and he finished it, left his chair to put the glass on the dresser, got out a cigarette and lit it, and turned to prop his backside against the dresser. "I'll tell you how it is," he said. "My situation's a little different. One thing, I was a boob to identify that stiff, but there he was, and in a case like that you can't stall, you've got to say yes or no, and I said yes. Now here we are. Miss Bonner said we might as well tell each other what we've told the cops, and I'll buy that, but my problem's not like yours. You see, I identified him as a guy named Bill Donahue I knew once."

He had already had six pairs of eyes, and with that he had them good. He grinned around at them.

"I said my situation's different. So I was stuck with that. So what I've told the cops. I've told them I'd seen him around a few times last spring, but it was kinda vague, I couldn't remember much about it except that once he came and wanted me to arrange a tap for him and I turned him down. They wanted to know whose wire he wanted tapped, and I tried to remember but couldn't. I said just for a fact I wasn't sure he had told me the name. So that's what I've told the cops, and that's what I'm telling you." He went to his chair and sat.

He still had the eyes. Wolfe's were half closed. He spoke. "I suggest, Mr. Amsel, that since talking with the police you've had time to jog your memory. Possibly you can be a little more definite about the occasions when you saw Donahue around last spring."

"Nothing doing. Just vague."

"Or the name of the man whose wire he wanted tapped?"

"Nope. Sorry."

"One thing occurs to me. Mr. Kerr has said he knew—to use his words—that 'they had two of the technicians singing.' Supposing that your memory has failed you on another detail, supposing that you did arrange the tap and have forgotten about it—just a supposition—wouldn't your situation be quite untenable if the technicians do remember it?"

"Just supposing."

"Certainly."

"Well, I've heard there were a lot of technicians around. I guess they're pretty scarce now. Supposing the ones doing the singing aren't the ones I used? Supposing the ones I used aren't going to sing?"

Wolfe nodded. "Yes, if I can suppose you can too. I understand your disinclination to tell us anything you haven't told the police, but I think we may reasonably ask this: did you mention this incident in your statement to the secretary of state?"

"What incident?"

"Your refusal to make the tap requested by Donahue."

"Why should I? We were told to report all taps. We weren't told to report refusals to make taps."

"You're quite right. Did you mention the name of Donahue at all in the statement?"

"No. What for?"

"Just so. You're right again, of course. I'm sure you'll agree, Mr. Amsel, that your contribution is even skimpier than Mr. Ide's. I don't know—"

The phone rang, and I went and got it. It was Lon Cohen. As I spoke with him, or rather, listened to him, Wolfe uncapped the second bottle of beer and poured. The guests were politely silent, as before. Again, after Lon had reported, he wanted the lowdown, and I promised to supply him with an eight-column headline as soon as we got one. I asked him to hold on a minute and told Wolfe, "Alan Samuels is a retired broker, Wall Street. He could live on Park Avenue but prefers the Bronx. His wife died four years ago. He has two sons and two daughters, all married. He gives money to worthy causes, nothing spectacular. Harvard Club. Director of the Ethical Culture Society. A year ago the governor appointed him a member of the Charity Funds Investigating Committee. I've got more, but it's not very exciting. Of course you note the item that might possibly be interesting."

"Yes. He's still on? Get the names of the members of that committee."

"Right." I went back to Lon. He said he'd have to send to the files, and did so, and then demanded some dope. I couldn't very well tell him that the other suspects were there in our room and Wolfe was doing his damnedest to find a crack to start a wedge in, so I gave him a human interest story about Nero Wolfe's behavior in the jug and other little sidelights. The list came, and he read it off while I wrote it down, and I told him not to expect the headline in time for the morning edition. I tore the sheet off of the memo pad and went and handed it to Wolfe, telling him, "That's it. Just five members, including the chairman."

He looked it over. He grunted. He looked at the guests. "Well. You may remember, from my statement, that Otis Ross is the chairman of the Charity Funds Investigating Committee. You have just heard that Alan Samuels is a member of that committee. So is Arthur M. Leggett. The names of the other two members are James P. Finch and Philip Maresco. It's a pity we have only three out of five. If it were unanimous it would be more than suggestive, it would be conclusive. Can you help us, Mr. Ide?"

Ide was looking uncomfortable. He pinched the skin over his Adam's apple, but that didn't seem to help, and he tried chewing on his lower lip, but since his teeth were a brownish yellow it didn't make him any handsomer. He spoke. "I said I wouldn't drag his name into this, but now it *is* in. I can't help it. You have named him."

"That makes four. Is there any point in leaving it to conjecture whether it was Finch or Maresco?"

"No. Finch."

Wolfe nodded. "That leaves only Maresco, and I hope he wasn't slighted. Mr. Amsel. Doesn't that name, Philip Maresco, strike a chord in your memory? At least a faint echo?"

Amsel grinned at him. "Nothing doing, Wolfe. My memory's gone very bad. But if you want my advice, just forget my memory. It's a cinch. If I was you I'd just take it for granted."

"Very well put. Satisfactory. Do you think it possible, ladies and gentlemen, that it was through coincidence that the five men whose wires Donahue wanted tapped were all members of that committee?"

They didn't think so.

"Neither do I. Surely it invites inquiry. Miss Bonner, how many competent operatives, not counting Miss Colt, are immediately available to you?"

She was startled. "Why . . . you mean now? Tonight?"

"Tonight or in the morning. What time is it, Archie?"

"Quarter past eleven."

"Then the morning will have to do. How many?"

She considered, rubbing her lip with a fingertip. I admit there was nothing wrong with her lips and she had good hands. "On my payroll," she said, "one woman and two men. Besides them, four women and three men whom I use occasionally."

"That makes ten. Mr. Ide?"

"What's this for?" Ide wanted to know.

"I'll explain. Now just how many."

"It depends on your definition of 'competent.' I have twelve good men on my staff. Eight or ten others might be available."

"Say twenty. That makes thirty. Mr. Kerr?"

"Call it nine. For an emergency I could scare up maybe five more, maybe six."

"Fifteen. That makes forty-five. Mr. Amsel?"

"I pass."

"None at all?"

"Well, I might. I've got no payroll and no staff. Wait till I hear the pitch, and I might."

"Then forty-five." Abruptly Wolfe got to his feet. "Now, if you'll permit me, I must arrange my mind. It shouldn't take long. I beg you to stay, all of you, to hear a suggestion I want to offer. And you must be thirsty. For me, Archie, a bottle of beer."

He moved his chair over near a window, turned it around, and sat, his back to the room.

They all took refills except Sally, who switched to coffee, and Ide, who declined with thanks. After phoning down the order I told them not to bother to keep their voices lowered, since nothing going on outside his head could disturb Wolfe when he was concentrating on the inside. They got up to stretch their legs, and Harland Ide went to Dol Bonner and asked her what her experience had been with women operatives, and Kerr and Amsel joined them and turned it into a general discussion. The drinks came and were distributed, and they went on exchanging views and opinions. You might have thought it was just a friendly gathering, and that nothing like a murder investigation, not to mention an official inquiry that might cost some of them their licenses, was anywhere near, unless you noticed their frequent glances at the back of Wolfe's chair. I gathered that with the men the consensus was that women were okay in their place, which I guess was the way cavemen felt about it, and all their male descendants. The question was, and still is, what's their place? I only hoped Wolfe wasn't getting any fleabite of a notion that Dol Bonner's place was in the old brownstone house on West Thirty-fifth Street.

When he finally arose and started turning his chair around I glanced at my wrist. Eight minutes to midnight. It had taken him half an hour to arrange his mind. He moved the chair back to its former position, and sat, and the others followed suit.

"We could hear it tick," Steve Amsel said.

Wolfe frowned at him. "I beg your pardon?"

"In your pan. The knocker."

"Oh. No doubt." Wolfe was brusque. "It's late, and we have work to do. I have reached a working hypothesis about the murder, and I want to describe it and suggest a collective effort. I intend to ask for full co-operation from all of you, and I expect to get it. I'll try to supply my share, though I have no organization to compare with Mr. Ide's and Mr. Kerr's. Archie, I must talk with Saul Panzer and it must be confidential. Can I do so from this room?"

"Good God no." I could have kicked him, asking such a dumb question in front of our fellow members. "Ten to one Groom would have it in ten minutes. And not from a booth in the hotel. You'll have to go out to one."

"Can you find one at this hour?"

"Sure. This is the City of Albany."

"Then please do so, and get him. Tell him I'll call

him at eight in the morning at his home. If he has other commitments ask him to cancel them. I need him."

"Right. As soon as we're through here."

"No. Now. If you please."

I could have kicked him again, but I couldn't start beefing in front of company. I went and got my hat and coat and beat it.

# VII

If you're no more interested than I was in how I spent the next day, Tuesday, you'll be bored stiff for the next four minutes.

There were happenings, but no developments that I was aware of. First about Monday night and Saul Panzer. Saul is the best there is and I would match him against all of the forty-five operatives our confreres had, all of them put together, but he ought to get home earlier and get to bed. I found a booth easy enough in a bar-and-grill, called the number, and got no answer. Going back to join the conference, and trying again later, was out. When Wolfe sends me on an errand he wants it done, and for that matter so do I. I waited five minutes and tried again, and then ten minutes and another try. That went on forever, and it was a quarter past one when I finally got him. He said he had been out on a tailing job for Bascom, and he was going to resume it at noon tomorrow. I said he wasn't, unless he wanted Wolfe and me indicted for murder and probably convicted, and told him to stand by for a call at eight in the morning. I gave him the highlights of the jolly day we had had, told him good night, returned to the hotel and up to room 902, and found Wolfe in bed sound asleep, in the bed nearest the window, with the window wide open and the room as cold as yesterday's corpse. From the open door to the bathroom I got enough light to undress by.

When I sleep I sleep, but even so I wouldn't have thought it possible that an animal of his size could turn out, get erect, and move around dressing and so on, without rousing me. In the cold, too. I would have liked to watch him at it. What got to me was the click as he turned the door knob. I opened my eyes, bounced up, and demanded, "Hey, where you going?"

He turned on the threshold. "To phone Saul."

"What time is it?"

"By the watch on your wrist, twenty past seven."

"You said eight o'clock!"

"I'll get something to eat first. Finish your rest. There's nothing to do, after I speak to Saul." He pulled the door shut and was gone. I turned over, worried a while about how he would squeeze into a booth, and went back to sleep.

Not as deep as before, though. At the sound of his key in the lock I was wide awake. I looked at my wrist: 8:35. He entered and closed the door, took off his hat and coat, and put them in the closet. I asked if he had got Saul, and he said yes and it was satisfactory. I asked how it had gone last night, had our fellow members agreed to co-operate, and he said yes and it was satisfactory. I asked what the program was for us, and he said there wasn't any. I asked him if that was satisfactory too, and he said yes. During this conversation he was removing duds. He stripped, with no visible reaction to the deep freeze, put on his pajamas, got into bed and under the blankets, and turned his back on me.

It seemed to be my turn, I was wide awake, it was going on nine o'clock, and I was hungry. I rolled out, went to the bathroom and washed and shaved, got dressed, having a little trouble buttoning my shirt on account of shivering, went down to the lobby and bought a *Times* and a *Gazette*, proceeded to the dining room and ordered orange juice, griddle cakes, sausage, scrambled eggs, and coffee. Eventually wearing out my welcome there, I transferred to the lobby and finished with the papers. There was nothing in them about the murder of William A. Donahue that I didn't already know, except a few dozen useless details such as the medical examiner's opinion that he had died somewhere between two and five hours before he got to him. It was the first time the *Gazette* had ever run pictures of Wolfe and me as jailbirds. The one of me was fair, but Wolfe's was terrible. There was one of Albert Hyatt, very good, and one of Donahue, which had evidently been taken after the scientists smoothed his face out. I went out for some air, turning up my overcoat collar against the wind, which was nearly as cold as room 902, and found that it was more fun to take a walk when you were out on bail. You want to go on and on and just keep going. It was after eleven o'clock when I got back to the hotel, took the elevator up to the ninth floor, and let myself into the deep freeze.

Wolfe was still in bed, and didn't stir when I entered. I stood and gazed at him, not tenderly. I was still considering the situation when there was a knock on the door behind me, a good loud one. I turned and opened it, and an oversized specimen was coming in, going to walk right over me. I needed something like that. I stiff-armed him good, and he tottered back and nearly went down.

"I'm a police officer," he barked.

"Then say so. Even if you are, I'm not a rug. What do you want?"

"Are you Archie Goodwin?"

"Yes."

"You're wanted at the district attorney's office. You and Nero Wolfe. I'm here to take you."

The correct thing to do would have been to tell him we'd consider it and let him know, and shut the door on him, but I was sorer at Wolfe than I was at him. There had been no good reason for sending me out to phone Saul until the conference had ended. It had been absolutely childish, when he returned from talking with Saul, for him to go back to bed without giving me any idea what was cooking. I had offered to split the blame fifty-fifty, but no, I was the goat and he was the lion. So I moved aside for the law to enter, and turned to see Wolfe's eyes open, glaring at us.

"That's Mr. Wolfe," I told the baboon.

"Get up and dress," he commanded. "I'm taking you to the district attorney's office for questioning."

"Nonsense." Wolfe's voice was colder than the air. "I have given Mr. Hyatt and Mr. Groom all the information I possess. If the district attorney wishes to come to see me in an hour or so I may admit him. Tell Mr. Groom he's an ass. He shouldn't have arrested me. Now he has no threat to coerce me with, short of charging me with murder or getting my bail canceled, and the one would be harebrained and the other quite difficult. Get out of here! No. Ha! No indeed. Archie, how did this man get in here?"

"Walked. He knocked, and I opened the door."

"I see. You, who can be, and usually are, a veritable Horatius. I see." His eyes moved. "You, sir. Were you sent for me only or both of us?"

"Both of you."

"Good. Take Mr. Goodwin. You could take me only by force, and I'm too heavy to lift. The district attorney can phone me later for an appointment, but I doubt if he'll get it."

The baboon hesitated, opened his mouth, shut it, and opened it again to tell me to come on. I went. Wolfe probably thought he had landed a kidney punch, but he hadn't. Since I was being kept off the program, kidding with a DA was as good a way to pass the time as any.

Another way of passing some time that had occurred to me was to offer to buy Sally Colt a lunch, but it was after two o'clock when the DA finally decided I was hopeless. I went to a drugstore and called Wolfe, told him the DA was hopeless, asked if he had any instructions, and was told no. I called Sally Colt and asked if she felt like taking in a movie, and she said she would love to but was busy and couldn't. *She* was busy. Fine. I did hope she would find some way of saving me from the electric chair. I started for the fountain counter for a sandwich and milk, remembered that this trip would go on the expense account, went and found the restaurant that Stanley Rogers had recommended, and ordered and consumed six dollars' worth of food, getting a receipt. The waiter told me where I could find a pool hall, and I walked to it, phoned to tell Wolfe where I was, sat and watched a while, got propositioned by a hustler, took him on at straight pool, and avoided getting cleaned only by refusing to boost the bets to the levels he suggested. He finally decided I was a piker and dropped me. By then it was going on seven o'clock, dinner time coming, but I had no intention of imposing myself on the occupant of room 902, so I mounted a stool to watch a pair of three-cushion sharks. They weren't Hoppes, but they were good. While one of them was lifting his cue for a massé, the cashier called to me that I was wanted on the phone. I took my time going. Let him wait.

"Hello."

"Hello, Mr. Goodwin?"

"Speaking."

"This is Sally Colt. I hated to say no to your invitation, I really did, but I had to. I don't suppose you feel like making it a dinner instead of a movie?"

I took time out for control. Only one person could have told her where I was. But it wasn't her fault. "Sure," I told her. "I eat every day. When?"

"Any time now. At the hotel?"

"No, there's a better place, just two blocks away. Henninger's. Shall we meet there in fifteen minutes?"

"It's a deal. Henninger's?"

"That's right."

"I'll be there. I'll tell Mr. Wolfe where we'll be in case he needs us."

"I'll phone him."

"No, I'll tell him, he's right here."

As I went for my coat and hat my feelings were too mixed to sort out. Cold rage. It was okay to make allowances for a genius, but this was too much. Curiosity. What the hell was he doing with her? Relief. At least he was up and dressed, unless his attitude toward women had done a complete somersault. Cheerfulness. Under almost any circumstances it's a pleasure to have a date with a good-looking girl. Expectation. Somewhere along the line she might see fit to tell me what my employer was up to.

She didn't. It was a very enjoyable meal, and before it was over I had decided that I would have to concede an exception to my verdict on she-dicks, but not a word about current affairs, and of course I wouldn't ask her. Wolfe had told her to lay off. I can't document that, but we got quite sociable by the time dessert and coffee came, and when a damsel smiles at me a certain way but steers clear of the subject she knows damn well is on top of my mind, she has been corrupted by someone. We were finishing our coffee and considering whether to move to a place down the street where there was a dance floor when the waiter came and told me I was wanted on the phone. I went.

"Hello."

"Archie?"

"Yeah."

"Is Miss Colt with you?"

"Yeah."

"Come to the room, and bring her."

"Yeah."

I returned to the table, told her we were wanted, got the check and paid it, and we left. The sidewalk was icy in spots and she took my arm, which seemed a little sissy for a working detective, but at least she didn't tug. At the hotel, when we got out at the ninth floor she went to her room, 917, to leave her things, and I waited in the hall for her. I had been told to bring her, and since that had been my only assignment for the day I wanted to carry it out properly. She rejoined me, we proceeded to 902, I opened the door with my key, and we entered.

The room was full of people.

"Well!" I said heartily, for I wasn't going to let my bitterness show in public. "Another party, huh?"

Wolfe was in the armchair toward the far wall. The writing table had been moved and was next to him, with papers on it. Dol Bonner was seated across the table from him. She was smirking. If you think I'm being unfair, that she wasn't really smirking but was merely showing no signs of misery, you're absolutely right. Wolfe nodded at me. "You may as well leave the door open, Archie. Mr. Groom and Mr. Hyatt are expected momentarily."

# VIII

My thought, as I put my hat and coat away, was that apparently the son-of-a-gun was going to try to pull one extra fancy and wrap it up in one package—not only put the finger on a murderer for Groom, but also mop up the hearing for Hyatt, as far as that bunch, including us, was concerned. It looked like a big order to fill without my help, but of course he had Dol Bonner. I thought it would be a pity if it turned out that she had knotted Donahue's necktie and he had to fall back on me.

I was glancing around, noting that Ide and Kerr and Amsel were in the chairs farthest away from Wolfe, with two empty ones up front for the expected company, when footsteps sounded in the hall, and I turned. Groom was in the lead. Evidently they had left their coats and hats downstairs.

Wolfe greeted them. "Good evening, gentlemen." He gestured. "Chairs for you."

They stood. Groom said, "I expected something like this. From you. You didn't say it was a convention."

"No, sir. I merely said that if you would come, and bring Mr. Hyatt, I was now prepared to add to my statement substantially and cogently. I prefer to have witnesses present." He gestured again. "If you will be seated?"

Groom looked at Hyatt, swiveled for a glance at me, moved through the gap between Kerr and Sally Colt, picked up one of the empty chairs and placed it against the wall, and sat. That way he had Wolfe and Dol Bonner on his right and the rest of us on his left, and couldn't be jumped from behind. Hyatt wasn't so particular. He didn't bother to move the chair but just sat, although five of us—Ide, Kerr, Amsel, Sally, and I —were in his rear.

"Let's hear it," Groom told Wolfe.

"Yes, sir." Wolfe shifted his chair to face him more directly. "A mass of detail is involved, but I won't cover it exhaustively now. You'll get it. First, the situation as it stood yesterday evening. In an ill-considered excess of zeal, you had arrested Mr. Goodwin and me. Therefore—"

"I know what the situation was."

"Not as I saw it. Therefore I had either to sit here and twiddle my thumbs, trusting to your skill and luck, or bestir myself. To begin with, I needed to learn, if possible, whether any of the other five people —those who had been in room forty-two with Mr. Goodwin and me—had had any association with Donahue. I invited them to this room for consultation, and they came. They—"

"I know they did. And today they wouldn't say what happened here. Not one of them. And Goodwin wouldn't. And you wouldn't."

"I will now. This will go faster, Mr. Groom, if you don't interrupt. They were here nearly four hours, and you won't need all of it. As soon as I learned that all of them had recognized the body, and so had known Donahue, and that their times of arrival at that building yesterday eliminated none of them, the inevitable assumption was that one of them had killed him, and I made it. I made it, and held it for about an hour, proceeding with our discussion, when I had to abandon it."

Groom started to speak and Wolfe showed him a palm. "If you please. Perhaps I should say 'suspended' instead of 'abandoned.' I suspended it because my attention was diverted to another quarter. I had noted it as an interesting point that seven people who had been associated with Donahue in connection with wiretapping had all been summoned to appear today. That it had been coincidence was against all probability, but it didn't have to be coincidence. It might have been so arranged purposely, for a comparison of their stories and even to bring them face to face.

"But no. It developed that that wouldn't do. None of us had mentioned Donahue's name in our statements to the secretary of state. Miss Bonner and Mr. Ide and I had all reported being duped by a man who had followed the same pattern with each of us, and our physical descriptions of him agreed, so we three might have been summoned by design to appear on the same day, but not Mr. Kerr and not Mr. Amsel. Mr. Kerr had merely reported tapping the wire of Arthur M. Leggett at Leggett's request. Mr. Amsel reported nothing—that is, nothing that could have linked him to Miss Bonner and Mr. Ide and me. Yesterday he identified Donahue as a man who had once asked him to make a tap and been refused, but he had made no mention of it in his statement to the secretary of state."

"You're getting nowhere fast," Groom declared. "You had all known him. One of you saw him there and killed him."

"But why were we all there?" Wolfe demanded. "That Miss Bonner and Mr. Ide and I had been brought together purposely was understandable, but not Mr. Kerr and Mr. Amsel. There was no connection, on the record; and yet they *were* connected, most significantly, since they too had had dealings with Donahue. By coincidence only? I didn't believe it. One of them, possibly, but surely not both. So my attention was diverted to the question, who had arranged for us all to be summoned to appear the same day? And simultaneously to another question, was there anything in common among the five men whose wires Donahue had wanted to tap? That suggested still another, why had he gone to five different detectives to arrange for the taps? Might it not have been because the five men *did* have something in common, and he didn't want that fact to be noted?"

Wolfe moved his eyes to Hyatt as if inviting an answer, but didn't get one. He returned to Groom. "My first question had to wait, since I couldn't very well call Mr. Hyatt and put it to him. The second was soon answered. I learned that four of the men whose wires had been tapped were members of the Charity Funds Investigating Committee, and had reason to suppose that the fifth one was also, embracing the entire committee. With that, I decided to describe the situation as I saw it to these ladies and gentlemen, and to enlist their co-operation. If it turned out that my surmise was wrong and one of them was in fact guilty, no harm would have been done; on the contrary, their reactions to my proposal might be indicative. I learned—"

"What proposal?" Groom demanded.

"I'm telling you. I learned that among them they had forty or more operatives in New York, and I could supply four or five. After describing the situation to them, I proposed that we put as many men as possible —and women—to work immediately. There were three main lines: one, the Hotel Marbury, where Donahue had lived; two, the background and interests and activities of Albert Hyatt, with emphasis on any discoverable connection with the Charity Funds Investigating Committee; and three—"

"You mean you suspected Hyatt of murder?"

"I mean I had formed a surmise I thought worth testing, and my confreres agreed with me. I have already put the question, who had arranged for all seven of us to appear on the same day? Mr. Hyatt was conducting the hearing. Another point, which is usually thought significant, but which you seem to have ignored, was that Mr. Hyatt was the last person, as far as was known, to see Donahue alive. Still another was that Hyatt had said that Donahue had told him that I had been given the name Donahue and that I had known the tap was illegal. I knew that either Donahue had lied or Hyatt was lying, and Donahue was dead."

Wolfe lifted his shoulders and dropped them. "What I suspected at that point is no longer important. The third line of investigation was to find evidence of former association between Hyatt and Donahue. My confreres made phone calls, and I made one myself. By ten o'clock this morning we had—how many operatives Miss Bonner?"

"By ten o'clock, thirty-four. By two this afternoon, forty-eight. Forty-two men and six women."

Steve Amsel suddenly exploded. "Too many detectives, Hyatt! Cancel our licenses! Too many!"

"Shut your trap!" Jay Kerr ordered him. "Wolfe's telling it."

Wolfe ignored them. "Reports started to reach us before one o'clock and have been arriving all afternoon, up to an hour ago, when we told the people in New York that we had enough for our purpose. Miss Bonner and Miss Colt took most of them, but the others helped. There was no important result from the first line of investigation, the Hotel Marbury. From the second, Hyatt's background and interests and activities, there was nothing conclusive, but much that is pregnant. Eighteen months ago derogatory information about the activities of fund-raising organizations began to appear in the press, and as the weeks passed it increased in volume and significance. A little more than a year ago Mr. Hyatt was retained as consulting counsel by a large fund-raising organization which had realized large profits, variously estimated at from one to three million dollars annually, from its operation. That was about the time that the governor set up the Charity Funds Investigating Committee, and Mr. Hyatt's client might reasonably expect to be a major target of that committee. There is some evidence that Mr. Hyatt approached two members of the committee in an effort to learn its plans—"

"What do you mean, 'some evidence'?" Groom demanded.

Wolfe tapped the papers on the table. "It's here waiting for you, but as I said, it is not conclusive. The committee members were not loquacious with our private operatives, but no doubt they will be more helpful with officers of the law. I merely give you this from our second line of investigation: that Mr. Hyatt was keenly interested in that committee and its plans. The results from our third line were more than pregnant, they were decisive, or close to it. It was of course the most promising, and thirty of the operatives were assigned to it. They were provided with pictures of Hyatt and Donahue from newspapers, and they found three people who had seen them together on two different occasions last spring—under circumstances that may fairly be described as furtive. I will not oblige Mr. Hyatt by naming the people and occasions and places, but that information is here." He tapped the papers again.

"And Mr. Hyatt has stated, in my hearing and yours, that he had never seen Donahue before yesterday morning. You asked if I suspect him of murder. I do now, yes. There are of course questions I am not prepared to answer, except with conjectures if you want them—for instance, the most important one, why did he arrange for all of us—he knew, of course, with whom Donahue had arranged for the taps—to appear before him on the same day? As a conjecture, because that was his best alternative, since we all had to be summoned for inquiry sooner or later, either in New York or in Albany, and he wanted us himself, not his colleague in New York. Having us all on the same day insured that we would all be at hand, to be called back in if occasion demanded it; and if things went smoothly he might well have intended to have us together before him and tell us magnanimously that, since our separate statements corroborated the assumption that we had all been imposed upon by a scoundrel, he would recommend no action against us."

Wolfe turned a hand over. "For he supposed, of course, that Donahue was safely out of the way, out of the state and not to be found. Unquestionably he had so arranged it. The situation held no great hazard for him. The fact that one of his clients was one of the targets of investigation of one of the governor's committees had no known connection with the investigation he was himself conducting, and he was confident that no such connection would be discovered or even suspected. Possibly he was even cocky, for he may have got, from the tapped wires, the information about the committee's plans and intentions that he needed. If so, he got a shattering blow when he answered his phone yesterday morning and was told that a man named Donahue wanted to see him about something urgent and confidential."

Wolfe's eyes went to Hyatt and back to Groom. "If you want another conjecture, what passed between Hyatt and Donahue in room thirty-eight yesterday, the most obvious one is that Donahue threatened to divulge the whole story—either as a screw for extortion, or because Donahue had learned that we seven had been called to appear together and suspected that he was to be made a scapegoat—and the obvious is often the best. Those questions, and others, are your concern, Mr. Groom, not ours. Our only concern was to show you that you were much too ready with a false assumption. As for Mr. Goodwin and me, I suppose you could successfully defend an action for false arrest, but I trust you have learned that it is infantile to take the word of a man as gospel merely because he is a special deputy of the secretary of state. Can the charge against us be dismissed tonight?"

"No. Not until court opens in the morning." Groom got up and went to the table and flattened his hand on the papers. He looked at the special deputy. "Mr. Hyatt, do you want to say anything?"

Hyatt was a lawyer. His back was to me, so I couldn't see his face, but I doubt if it was showing anything much. "Except," he said, "that I deny all of Wolfe's allegations and implications regarding me, and that I'll hold him responsible for them, no. I have nothing to say here and now." He got up and started for the door. Groom made no move to stop him, and couldn't be expected to, at least until he had inspected the papers.

Steve Amsel called after him, "Too many detectives, Hyatt!"


**I X**


Yesterday afternoon I was in the office with Wolfe, discussing a little job we had taken on, when the phone rang and I answered it.

"Nero Wolfe's office, Archie Goodwin speaking."

"This is Dol Bonner. How are you?"

"Better than ever."

"Good. May I speak to Mr. Wolfe?"

"Hold it, I'll see." I covered the transmitter and turned and told Wolfe. He made a face, hesitated, and reached for his phone. I kept mine to my ear, since I was supposed to unless he told me otherwise.

"Yes, Miss Bonner? Nero Wolfe."

"How are you?"

"Well, thank you."

"I'm glad I got you. Of course you've heard the news?"

"I don't know. What news?"

"The jury reached a verdict at noon. They found Hyatt guilty of first-degree murder."

"So. I hadn't heard. To be expected, surely."

"Of course. Why I called, Harland Ide phoned me an hour ago. He thinks it would be a little barbarous to celebrate a man's conviction for murder, and I agree, so that's not the idea, but he suggested that we should show our appreciation to you somehow. Anyway, the secretary of state has reported the results of the hearing and we're all going to keep our licenses, so we could celebrate that. Mr. Ide thought we might have a little dinner for you, just the seven of us, and wanted to know if I approved, and I said I did. Just now he called again and said that Mr. Kerr and Mr. Amsel liked the idea, and he asked me to propose it to you. Any evening you choose next week—or as for that, any other week. We hope you will, and of course Mr. Goodwin. And of course Miss Colt."

Silence. I was watching Wolfe's face. His lips were pressed tight.

"Are you on, Mr. Wolfe?"

"Yes, I'm on. I rarely accept invitations to meals."

"I know. This isn't a meal, it's a tribute."

"Which it would be churlish to decline. Mr. Goodwin thinks I *am* churlish, but I don't. I am merely self-indulgent. I offer a counter-suggestion. I too feel appreciation, for the efficient and effective co-operation I received. I suggest that instead of dining at some restaurant, which I suppose is intended, you people come to my house for dinner. Any evening next week except Thursday."

"But that would be turning it wrong side up!"

"Not at all. I said I feel appreciation too."

"Well . . . shall I ask Mr. Ide? And the others?"

"I wish you would."

"All right. I'll let you know."

And she did. In less than an hour. It's all set for next Wednesday evening. I'm looking forward to it. It will be a treat to see Fritz's face when he sees Dol Bonner, seated at Wolfe's right, aim her caramel-colored eyes at him under her long dark lashes.

As for the fifty-fifty split on the blame for our

wiretap, that's still under discussion off and on. And as for my being left off the program that day in the City of Albany, that needed no discussion. Since all the work had to be done by the 48 operatives in New York and there was nothing I could contribute, why deal me in? Especially since I could be useful as a diversion for Groom and the DA.

# The World of
# Rex Stout

Now, for the first time ever, enjoy a peek into the life
of Nero Wolfe's creator, Rex Stout, courtesy of the
Stout Estate. Pulled from Rex Stout's own archives,
here are rarely seen, never-before-published memora-
bilia. Each title in "The Rex Stout Library" will offer
an exclusive look into the life of the man who gave
Nero Wolfe life.

## Three for the Chair

Reviewers disagreed over the merits of Rex Stout's
*Three for the Chair.* Anthony Boucher, in *The New
York Times*, found it "one of the best of Stout's three-
somes." But Julian Symons, in London's *Sunday
Times*, made the suggestion—blasphemous to most
devotees of Nero Wolfe—that it was time for Stout to
kill off the great detective! Both reviews are repro-
duced here.

Extract from

# THE SUNDAY TIMES
## LONDON

# CRIME STORIES
## By JULIAN SYMONS

LIKE some vestigial limb, the Great Detective lingers on, although the social conditions that encouraged his omniscient amateurism have long since vanished.

Consider, for example, Mr. Rex Stout's Nero Wolfe, that Gilbert Harding of detection who entered the ring as heavyweight contestant for criminal honours some thirty years ago equipped with a fine set of prejudices, including a particular one against moving out of his old brownstone house on West 35th Street. In those days ever, new Nero Wolfe story was a delight, a fresh exercise of Mr. Stout's ingenuity in providing clues that would enable Nero to solve problems without moving further than the plant rooms on the roof.

That was long ago. The three longish short stories in "**Three for the Chair**" find Wolfe making a trip to the Adirondacks to cook trout for an ambassador, and tamely allowing himself to be taken the 160 miles from New York to Albany for an investigation into wire-tapping. "Three for the Chair" offers one murder method that is new to me, but is otherwise a sad comment on past glories. A peripapetic Nero Wolfe has really no reason for existence. Could not Mr. Stout arrange for him to pass away after an excess of salmon mousse and blueberry pie?

# Criminals
# At Large

By ANTHONY BOUCHER

THOSE who, like me, firmly believe that most mystery novels of 50 to 70,000 words could be more effective as novelettes of 20 to 30,000 can normally find the proper concise length (at least in book form) only once a year, in the annual "Nero Wolfe Threesome." But so far this year (the gods of terseness be praised) we've had an earlier novelette collection by Henry Kane, and this week volumes by Rex Stout and Richard S. Prather.

**THREE FOR THE CHAIR** (Viking, $2.95) is one of the best of Stout's threesomes, marred indeed by hardly anything save its inaccurate title (the whole point of one story is that its killer is *not* for the chair). The situations and solutions are unusually good ones; and the stories are rich in unexpected Wolfiana: Wolfe preparing brook trout Montbarry (his own invention), Wolfe under arrest for the first time, Wolfe calling once upon the Secretary of State and once upon a band of four dozen operatives to pull out his chestnuts for him, Wolfe even going so far as to make a sort of professional sheep's eyes at private detective Dol Bonner. . . . As I've often said before, it's hard to find three novels as satisfying as these treble groups of novelettes.